A FRIEND LIKE ME

Melanie Sinclair's career in journalism distances her from home, family, and Calvert Robson, a partner in her father's law firm who suspects his freewheeling lifestyle is the cause of Melanie choosing foreign assignments. When Melanie learns of her father's ill health, she accepts a television newsreading job. Then she discovers that Cal is moving his business out of the village and opening offices in Newcastle, where he also intends to live. Is she too late in discovering what Cal really means to her?

PIA WALTON

A FRIEND LIKE ME

Complete and Unabridged

LINFORD
Leicester

First published in Great Britain in 2003

First Linford Edition
published 2005

British Library CIP Data

Walton, Pia
    A friend like me.—Large print ed.—
Linford romance library
    1. Love stories
    2. Large type books
    I. Title
    823.9'2 [F]

ISBN 1–84617–109–1

Published by
F. A. Thorpe (Publishing)
Anstey, Leicestershire

Set by Words & Graphics Ltd.
Anstey, Leicestershire
Printed and bound in Great Britain by
T. J. International Ltd., Padstow, Cornwall

This book is printed on acid-free paper

1

Melanie Sinclair flung three suitcases, a collection of travel bags and a hotch-potch of other paraphernalia into the Denton Park Estate's station wagon and turning, she caught a glimpse of her mother's doleful expression and sighed.

'I'm only moving to Aunt Isobel's house over on Parson's Green, Mother, which is hardly the ends of the earth, as you so dramatically put it.'

'I know, Melanie. There's just something so final about you packing all your belongings and not living with your father and me any longer.'

'Realistically, I haven't lived in Juniper Cottage since my first foreign assignment, so this is not such a big deal. Come on, Mum, hop in the car and help me unpack this lot at the other end. Tell you what, you'll be glad I

1

moved out of Juniper Cottage before my holiday's over.'

Understanding how her mother felt was easy. It was usual for a daughter teetering on the edge of thirty to leave home, but more commonly with a husband in tow and that was the crux of this matter.

There was no husband, or the faintest glimmer of one in sight.

Melanie stopped the car.

'I'll be ten minutes away from you and Dad.'

'It's not the distance, pet, it's the very idea of you still being in King's Denton yet not having your meals with us. Your father will miss you. And while it was good of Aunt Isobel to leave the house to you, I only wish she'd given some thought to the consequences of her misguided action.'

Melanie laughed.

'If you're worried I'll follow in her footsteps and become a dyed-in-the-wool spinster, forget it, Mother. You know I like men too much for that.'

Emily Sinclair laughed and was in better spirits when she left her daughter to settle in, but only after extricating a promise from her to have dinner with her father and herself that evening.

'It's tough on them having no family at home now, no grandchildren and no sign of any,' Mel murmured to herself later as she gazed from a bedroom window overlooking the village green.

Such a typically Victorian house, Mel mused, raising her eyes to the high ceiling, casting a glance at the charming, old tiled fireplace, and moving to the bed, she affectionately ran her hand along the length of her aunt's pretty blue and cream patchwork quilt.

'You wanted me to have this house for some reason, Isobel, and it's strange that you've bequeathed it to me when, for the first time in my life, I feel a strong need for a place of my own to come back to, a door of my own to open and at times close, to shut out the rest of the world.'

Melanie didn't need to be reminded

by anyone of her driving ambition, of having sacrificed more than she cared to dwell on at this point in her life. She had no axe to grind, had planned and plotted her career in journalism long before her three-year stint at Newcastle University and worked all out to achieve the success she sought, first as a successful journalist and later, a dedicated foreign correspondent for a television company.

'So why the sudden heart-searching introspection?' she muttered.

Gazing from the window to the street below, Ben Robson's old estate car reminded her that it was time for its return, and maybe spending an hour or so with Tessa, who was sure to bring her up to date with the King's Denton news. It would snap her out of this strange, brooding mood.

After parking the car in the big stable, Mel strolled across the Denton Park estate in the warm, end-of-July sunshine and, nearing her friend's studio, thought of the comparative pleasantness of Tessa's life to her own. A successful artist these days, Tessa was married to a man she loved and who loved her.

Melanie laughed aloud at the sound of Charlie's bark. She had forgotten Tessa's spaniel, the four-legged member of the family who followed his mistress almost everywhere. And then, for her sins, Mel mused, poor Tessa Maitland had been lumbered with a friend like me!

'Hi, what's new?'

Her quiet voice jolted her friend out of a deep study and Mel watched as a slow smile spread across Tessa's pretty face.

'Mel! Why didn't somebody tell me you were home?' Tessa exclaimed. 'And, this morning, well may you ask what's new.'

'So, what is new?' Mel repeated, instantly intrigued.

'Come in. I'll put the kettle on and tell you the most staggering offer that just fell out of the sky this morning.'

Charlie was on his feet and sniffing the biscuit tin before the first drops of water hit the kettle, making Mel laugh as, patiently, she glanced about her. The purpose-built studio was a gem and all down to Tessa who had known precisely what she wanted and always had, artistically speaking.

'Love the painting of a stretch of flowers by the roadside, Tessa.'

'We were on our way back from Newcastle when Calvert pointed the drift of poppies out to me and I couldn't wait to get back to the studio to get it on canvas. I wished you could have made it to Grandma's eighty-fourth birthday party, by the way.'

It sounded to Mel as if Tessa's brother, Cal, had a great time at the party if he'd commented on the attraction of wild flowers edging a motorway! Nonetheless, it was gratifying to know Cal had some beauty in his soul.

'Can you believe Giles Shepherd has

negotiated an exhibition of my work in America?'

'Wow! That is good news, but where?' Mel asked.

'Washington DC. Apparently an American friend of his saw some of my work in London and wants to show it in his Georgetown gallery. I'm flattered and excited, Mel, but at the same time, it's a bit scary.'

'So, when is this exhibition happening and what does Josh have to say about his wife flitting off to the States?'

'We've talked about it and, naturally, he's delighted for me, says I must go, can't miss a chance like this, but I'm not so sure.'

'For goodness' sake, Tessa, this is a once-in-a-lifetime opportunity.'

'James'll be going back to school after the summer holiday about that time, so one of us will have to be here for him and if Josh stays here, then I'll be there, on my own, in Georgetown.'

'Nonetheless, this is too good an offer to turn down, and you didn't for a moment think I wouldn't go with you?' Mel said, laughing at Tessa's look of wide-eyed incredulity.

'Would you really do that? Oh, if only you would, but it's impossible. There's your job to consider, Mel, and that's far more important.'

'If you want me there, I'll find a way without putting my job in jeopardy. Think back to my first break. You were sixteen when you helped me land that job and I'll be with you all the way for yours.'

Charlie barked at the muffled growl of an approaching car and Tessa glanced at Melanie.

'That sounds like Cal's car.'

Why the mention of his name should instantly make Mel's heart beat faster annoyed her. Tessa's brother was history, not even a love affair, but more of a teenage learning curve, long over and painfully done with.

'Hi, Mel,' Cal greeted her. 'This is an

unexpectedly pleasant surprise. I hear you've already moved into Isobel's house.'

Tessa looked surprised.

'Have you really? Why didn't you tell me you were moving in today? Oh, of course, that's why you needed the big old car. Josh and I should've helped you.'

'There was virtually nothing to move. As you know, the house is fully furnished and any changes I want to make can be done any time.'

'So when is the housewarming party, gorgeous?' Cal asked breezily.

'As Aunt Isobel's solicitor and friend, don't you think a party in her home at this time would be, to say the least, uncaring?'

'Not in the slightest. Isobel Crowther loved parties, would've loved the very idea of you having a housewarming in the house she loved almost as much as she loved you.'

That Cal's few words should make her eyes damp didn't make sense.

Mel stood up.

'Give Josh my love, Tessa, and if you would tell your father his old bus was greatly appreciated today, I would be grateful.'

Calvert was on his feet in an instant.

'I'll run you back to Parson's Green, Mel.'

'Thank you, but I'd rather walk, and a freewheeling lothario, such as yourself, wouldn't want to be seen with anyone straight-laced, even if she was a friend. Think of your reputation, Calvert,' she reminded him sweetly.

'So, come off your high horse, Melanie Sinclair, and I'll run you back. There are things I need to talk to you about.'

'Such as?' she enquired crustily.

'We can't talk here. Tessa is busier than ever with this American show stuff and Josh will be at his computer.'

'Come back tomorrow, Mel, and we'll have tea together,' Tessa said.

'Better still, Tessa, take the day off and we'll go into Newcastle. I need to buy some new clothes. I'll phone you later.'

They were almost in King's Denton before Cal said, 'You're never here, that's always been the trouble.'

'You know where to address letters when I'm . . . '

'I wasn't talking business, Mel.'

'What else have we to talk about? Your love life continues to flourish, or so I'm told. Your current girlfriends are hard to keep pace with.'

'Remember your graduation party in The Three Horseshoes by the river? We had some great times together,' Cal reminded her quietly.

'For me the best party at that pub was when we celebrated my first big article. That was quite a summer.'

'And quite a party. We danced the night away and half the gang pooh-poohed the ferry ride home and swam across the river.'

They were laughing when they reached her new home which didn't seem at all new to her. It had always

11

been her other home, just as Aunt Isobel had been as close as her own mother.

'You'll have a lot of happy memories about this house, too,' Cal commented.

'Yes, Cal, but there are no ghosts here for me. If one did show up, it would be a friendly one.'

She felt a justifiable and warm sense of pride in owning Isobel's beautiful house. It was an elegant, old stone building and if the interior reflected the age of its former owner, here again, the antique furniture had been carefully, lovingly collected over the years.

Calvert sat in a comfortable wing chair at one side of the fireplace and stretched out his legs.

'I wondered if you had any idea that your father was seriously thinking of retiring,' he said out of the blue.

'Heavens, no. Is he really? I hadn't a clue. What's more, I'm fairly sure he hasn't breathed a word of it to Mother.'

'Your father has suggested that when he leaves the firm, I should pick up the reins and I need to know if you have any objection to this.'

Cal looked for her immediate reaction and, surprised at her nodded, tacit agreement, he leaned forward in his chair.

'Knowing there has been a Sinclair in that King's Denton lawyer's office since time immemorial, you're not going to raise the slightest objection to a brash, young interloper you could never altogether trust?'

'And still self-assertive, but age seems to be softening the edges,' she said with a smile. 'It's true, the family has been here a long time,' she added, thinking the news of her father's retirement hadn't shaken her as much as Cal's willingness to shoulder such daunting responsibility.

'So, Mel, you would raise no objection to me running the show if your father retires sometime next year?'

Melanie shook her head again.

'There was a time when my father

had high hopes of me entering the profession, but when he discovered your latent interest in law, well, you've always been like a son to him,' she ended lamely.

Calvert gazed steadily at her.

'That's good to know, but although we grew up almost as one family, I haven't thought of you in a sisterly light for some time,' he said softly.

If the message implicit in his remark wasn't lost on her, she nevertheless chose to ignore it. She was not about to be pigeonholed along with his string of hero-worshipping girlfriends. She'd been there.

'You've heard about Tessa's amazing Georgetown show?'

Nor was her sudden change of topic lost on Cal who answered, 'Yes, but I'm not surprised. She's doing very well, getting talked about in the art world, and if that drink's still on offer, Mel, I'd like a beer.'

'Talented and happily married with a little boy she adores,' Mel said on her

14

way to the kitchen, returning with a can of chilled lager.

'Isn't that something every woman wants, a happy marriage and children of her own? I know you always wanted brothers and sisters. Isn't there a handsome television announcer or photo-journalist in your life?'

He grinned at her and raised the lager.

'Cheers, Mel.'

'The trouble is, I would want a one-woman man, someone who loved and wanted only me and on a long-term basis, but from my albeit limited experience, that isn't in the nature of the beast.'

'You're saying that if you found this perfect specimen, you'd give up your foreign assignments, stop chasing off to every strife-torn country on the hunt for a story and settle down to married life? Come on, Mel, be truthful. You're talking to Calvert.'

'About as believable as you accepting my father's challenge, eh?'

'Ah, that's different. Your father trusts me and I would never betray his trust. I've already given him my solemn promise to keep the Sinclair flag flying here in King's Denton and as little faith as you have in me, Mel, you must know I'd never break my word.'

She couldn't miss the angry flash in his eyes or the censure in his voice and it hurt her that their few discussions on any subject lately had to end in point scoring, bickering or disharmony of one sort of another. Yet it was sweet and old-fashioned of him to think that every woman longed to be married and have children.

Calvert drained the last of his beer and pushed himself out of the armchair.

'Why do you do that?' he demanded.

'Sorry? What's that?'

'Go out of your way to annoy me. You are always perfectly civil to other men, yet have this perverse need to be uncivil to me.'

'You're becoming very sensitive in

16

your old age, Cal. You and I have always squabbled,' she said, laughing when he reached for her hand and, unceremoniously, hauled her out of the chair.

'Do I have to keep reminding you that we are not brother and sister?' he asked, his arms encircling her waist. 'Or maybe more than words are needed to convince you,' he added, bending, his lips brushing hers.

Melanie wondered if he could hear her heart thumping.

'Right, you've made your point, Cal. I'm not your sister,' she said shakily, her mind working overtime, looking for what lay behind his new, decidedly more unsisterly interest in her.

His fingers gently tapped her forehead.

'I can almost hear this calculator of yours working overtime.'

She took a slow, deep breath and tried to keep her voice level.

'When I get to it, I doubt if the bottom line will hold any surprises.'

His fingers swept from her brow to

caress her cheek.

'Still on your guard, eh? So, what're you doing for dinner tonight?'

'Juniper Cottage with Mum and Dad.'

'You moved out of the cottage a few hours ago and your mother's missing you already?' Calvert laughed. 'And when d'you leave for goodness knows where again?'

'Unless I'm called for something special, I could be here for a week, maybe ten days.'

'Good. Thanks for the beer, Mel. See you.'

'Thanks for bringing me up to date about the old firm and unravelling our relationship for me,' she added with a touch of irony.

'That was pure, unadulterated pleasure, Mel. I'll be in touch.'

The laughter in his voice stayed long after the front door slammed shut.

Changing from jeans and cotton top to a dress her mother would more readily approve of, Melanie stopped and looked into Aunt Isobel's large bedroom mirror. She wasn't even Cal's type, certainly didn't look the part with flushed cheeks, brown eyes, long dark hair that shot back into a curl at the slightest breath of air.

'That apart, it isn't all mediocrity,' she told herself, twisting and turning. 'My figure's good, better than average, even if I don't remotely fit into the long-legged, golden-haired category of female that Calvert Benjamin Robson shows a preference for.'

All she had done differently today was move into the house on the village green and, out of the goodness of his heart, Cal had dropped in to wish her well in her new home, as friends do. And it was good of him to ask her opinion about her father's impending retirement.

She sat on the edge of the bed and thought of how he'd kissed her countless times, but that was in the past, long ago and kid's stuff when, with Tessa, they'd constantly been together, an inseparable trio. Those were her star-struck teenage years she'd rather forget.

Yet, how could she forget the long, golden summer days they'd messed about in canoes or swam in the river and around twilight would wander back to Denton Hall to throw together a meal for themselves in the big kitchen with their favourite music playing, too loud for the older generation to be within earshot, Mel reflected, dreamily.

Falling in love at sixteen had been an agonising experience, taking a long, painful time to overcome. Small wonder Cal's impromptu show of affection today had completely thrown her. She slipped her dress over her head and, this time, smiled at her reflection. Knowing how little it would mean to him, she was no longer a vulnerable schoolgirl and, brotherly or not, she could cope with the odd kiss.

★ ★ ★

'You should have a house-warming party, Melanie, shouldn't she, Harvey?' Emily Sinclair said, placing hot vegetable dishes on the table. 'I would willingly see to all the food, do the flower arranging and things like that. You need only scribble a list of people you want to come and I'd see to the invitations, too, Melanie.'

'Thanks, I know you would. The thing is, I'd have to be here on the day, but if I'm suddenly called away, you know I have to drop everything and go.'

'I just wish we could turn the clock back to the days when you worked for Keeble Willoughby on the local newspaper and reported on local parish council meetings, weddings and such like. At least we knew where you were in those days.'

'Horseradish sauce, Mel? And have you seen Calvert since you came back?' Harvey asked, cleverly changing the topic.

'He called earlier to wish me

21

happiness in Isobel's house which I thought sweet of him.'

'I'm sure you'll agree when the time comes for me to retire that I couldn't leave the business in a safer pair of hands than his.'

'Well, you should leave your office while you're still fit and able to enjoy life, Daddy. And nobody's a better judge of character, so you'll know whether Calvert Robson's the right man to pick up the reins.'

'It's more than that. I like Cal. There's something straight and inherently true about that lad. He's a chip off the Robson block.'

'Still, it's a pity he isn't married and settled in King's Denton. We all like Calvert, Harvey. It's the inordinate time he's taking to decide on a wife that I find puzzling,' Emily stated, stabbing a tiny new potato.

'Youthful high spirits, that's all. He'll settle down when he's good and ready. And when the time comes to choose a wife, you can be sure Cal will make a wise choice. She'll be the right woman for him.'

'And by that time, Dad, with his phenomenal experience, who will be better qualified?' Melanie added drily, making her father laugh.

'And if he doesn't pick the right one, I know Sally and Ben Robson will be bitterly disappointed. Apart from being at the head of our law firm in the near future, Cal is heir to the Denton Park Estate and from what I've seen of his female companions lately, they might be considered beautiful by some, but they leave a lot to be desired as a fitting wife for him, to my way of thinking.'

Melanie and her father listened without demur to the well-trodden ground of Emily Sinclair's pet hobby horse, until Harvey asked, 'Had you anyone suitable in mind, dear?'

'Well, I've often thought that if Melanie stopped gallivanting around the world and made an effort to be at least civil to Calvert occasionally, he would see that while she might not be as beautiful as some, she's more than capable of being mistress of the Hall. You would be a real asset to a man like Calvert Robson.'

'Thanks, Mum, I'm sure there must be a compliment in there somewhere,' Mel managed to say before bursting into a fit of laughter with Harvey, unable to hold out any longer, joining in the hilarity.

Her mother didn't understand the long-held truce that existed between Cal and herself, so Mel couldn't blame her for both making matrimonial bullets and firing them in her direction with tedious regularity. That apart, the love in Juniper Cottage more than made up for her mother's oblique reminders that she wanted grandchildren.

At the first note of the door chimes, Harvey was on his feet saying, 'That'll be Calvert. He said he might call. He's in court in the morning.'

'This will mean they'll be closeted in the study until goodness knows when,'

Emily groused, yet she gave Cal a warm, friendly smile as he joined them. 'If you'd told me you were calling here, we could've had dinner together, but you might like coffee and a roast beef sandwich.'

'Thanks, but I had something to eat with Tessa and Josh earlier. Hi, Melanie.'

She smiled.

'Hi, Cal. Been working out, I see,' she replied, figuring he might've told her there was a case he intended going through with her father this evening.

'However did you guess?' Cal laughed.

The wet hair made it look six shades darker. How could she not observe? And he was wearing T-shirt and white shorts showing tanned arms, legs and overall view of a physically fit, fine specimen of manhood.

'Shot in the dark. I hear you've come to work.'

He nodded.

'For my sins. Give me half an hour with your father, Mel, and I'll walk you back to Parson's Green.'

But when an hour had gone by without a sound being heard from the men in the study and talk of Tessa's amazing introduction into America's artistic world was reaching near exhaustion point, Melanie stood up and kissed her mother's cheek.

'It's getting late and as you say, they could be in there for hours. Goodnight, Mum. Tell Cal I waited as long as I could.'

The words had a familiar, discordant ring to them. The story of my life crossed her mind, possibly would've been if she hadn't swung her attention, focusing it exclusively on her career when she did.

'Give them another quarter of an hour, Melanie. They can't take longer than that and I'm sure Calvert won't like the idea of you walking home alone.'

'Don't worry, Mum, I'll be fine and I want to make an early start tomorrow. Tessa and I are going into Newcastle to do some clothes shopping. Why don't you come with us?'

'I'd love to, pet, but your father asked me to attend a local trade function on his behalf and I can hardly refuse when he and Calvert are just about deluged with work lately.'

As she walked back to the cottage, she heard the voice call to her, but decided not to stop.

'That has to be one for the record, Calvert Robson running after me.'

She slowed her pace, marginally.

A hand grabbed her shoulder and she swung round.

'What, you're out of breath? A great, strapping lad like you? And you're wearing all the right kit, so you have me at a disadvantage, Cal.'

'I will, one of these fine days, Melanie,' he threatened ominously.

'Will what?'

'Have you at a disadvantage, one day when you're not feeling quite so smart and sassy.'

'Don't hold your breath,' she quipped,

laughing at him.

It was a balmy, summer evening as they strolled along the riverside towards Parson's Green, the waxing moon silvering the gently-flowing river and lighting their way home.

Passing their favourite pub, Cal said, 'What exactly did Tessa tell you about this American exhibition of hers?'

'She's thrilled. Thinks it's a great opportunity, but wasn't keen on travelling alone, so I said I'd go with her. What does Josh think of her swanning across the Atlantic so soon after their wedding?'

'The poor man's madly in love. In his befuddled state, he thinks she's perfect and can do no wrong. What can I say?'

'That's something you wouldn't let a wife of yours do?'

'Married to someone like you, I'd leave the children with either your mother or mine and insist on going with you. I wouldn't dare let you out of my sight in case you met up with a news crew and went off with them on another of your hair-raising, journalistic exploits.'

It was the tenderness in his voice when he spoke of children that surprised her, but she reminded herself that her reaction would be pretty much the same as that of any of his female companions, given a stroll home by the river with Calvert Robson's hand holding hers.

'You make my work sound one long, glamorous adventure, Cal, certainly more attractive than, in reality, it is. And what a blessed relief for you to know you'll never find yourself in the unenviable position of being married to this single-minded career woman,' she said, light-heartedly.

When they stopped at her door, she turned the key in the lock and smiled at her gallant friend.

'Good-night, Cal. Thanks for seeing me safely home,' she whispered, and quietly closed the door behind her.

2

Melanie brought her car to a standstill outside Briar Rose Cottage and was pleasantly surprised to see it and the cottage adjoining, conversion completed, now a spacious single dwelling and a delightful home for Tessa, Josh and little James, Josh's son.

'Hi, Mel,' Tessa called.

'Hello, Aunt Melanie,' James chimed in, climbing into the car, a posy of wild scabious and silky-looking grasses clutched tightly in his hand.

'Now, let me guess, James. You've picked that pretty bunch for your grandma. Right?'

James gave her a self-satisfied smile and nodded.

'Grandma Fenwick. She's pretty, like Mummy.'

'He's like his father, Mel, with an eye for the ladies,' Tessa muttered.

'Have fun in Newcastle, Mel, but see you take special care of my girl,' Josh called out from an open window.

Mel waved back, her mind on Tessa's stepson who had just referred to his stepmother as mummy. And knowing how Tessa loved Josh's little boy, it must be comforting to know that particularly tricky hurdle had been cleared successfully. She smiled at his ridiculous instruction to take care of Tessa. Still, she could make allowances for a man so obviously in love and probably hating the idea of being separated from her.

Half an hour later, with a list of instructions as long as her arm from Grandma, and copious hugs and kisses from James for both Melanie and Tessa, the girls headed for the city centre.

'You must be finding family life a bit of a hassle without the help of your mother's housekeeper,' Mel said, glancing at Tessa's flushed cheeks.

'It's true, I do miss Molly, but with or without a housekeeper, I'll have to learn how to cope with the daily grind much sooner than I thought necessary,' Tessa replied, a secretive little smile on her lips.

Intrigued, Mel angled her head and raised her brows. They were on the up-escalator, about to join the other shoppers in the ladies' fashion department of one of the bigger stores in Newcastle when Tessa continued.

'Cal interrupted our conversation about my paintings going to Georgetown just when I was on the point of telling you that I'm pregnant.'

'What?' Mel shrieked, stumbling on the top step and going headlong towards an eye-catching display of summer dresses.

Quickly, she straightened up, brushed a hand over her smart black suit and caught Tessa laughing at her.

'Congratulations, and I don't usually do handstands on such occasions, but for you . . . '

Words were unnecessary she felt, giving Tessa a big hug. Looking at her friend's wistful gaze towards the attractive summer fashions, it struck Mel that they were in the wrong department. She sidled up to Tessa.

'Did the doctor tell you when the baby was due?'

'Yes and I've already worked out that I'll be five months when we leave for Washington.'

'So, you're fit and well and there's nothing to be concerned about?'

'Better than the first three months, Mel. The morning sickness should just about be over then, and my doctor says I'll be feeling on top of the world.'

'That's a load off our minds then. I suppose the baby was the reason you felt nervous about travelling alone and, of course, why else would Josh ask me to take special care of you today?'

'Make allowances for him, Mel. He's so thrilled about the baby, he's on cloud nine.'

'Come on then, let's go to the maternity section and look for some really smart gear for the five-months-pregnant lady,' Mel teased, making Tessa smile a little wider.

'Right. I should look my best in a place like Georgetown. Grandma loved living there. You know how she eulogises about her life in America and the people. She couldn't believe I was loathe to venture there alone. Thought I was mad to miss such a glorious opportunity.'

The girls were nearing the end of their Newcastle shopping centre circuit, and had reached a stage where they couldn't possibly carry another bag, when Melanie suggested lunch at The Quayside.

'The riverside restaurants are very expensive, and we've already spent a small fortune on my lovely new clothes,' Tessa reminded her, feeling more than slightly guilty at having spent so much on herself.

'We're doing it in style today. My treat before I go back to facing the stark reality of working life next Monday,'

Mel insisted, raising her hand to flag down a taxi.

Lunch by the Tyne was a perfect choice. It was a warm, brilliantly sunny day with a gentle breeze, the incoming tide creating sparkling ripples in its surge to meet the river.

'Well, you wanted style and this has to be it,' Tessa remarked, her eyes raking the sumptuous restaurant.

'I didn't think it would be quite as popular as this. Coming on spec, I suppose we should think ourselves lucky there was a vacant table.'

'I'm just grateful for this chair and would cheerfully have waited an hour or more for the table,' Tessa joked.

'An impressive place, even exciting,' Mel murmured, more to herself as she looked round at the cosmopolitan scene.

'Look over there.'

Taken completely by surprise, Tessa angled her head in the direction of a window table at the far end of the room.

'That looks remarkably like Cal, but I've no idea who the woman is.'

'It is Calvert.' Mel replied quietly, instantly averting her eyes and, not without a touch of cynicism, thinking the fair-haired lady stood a good chance of being his latest conquest.

Mel just hoped she would one day find a way not to care with whom Calvert Robson ate his lunch, dinner or, come to that, breakfast.

'She'll be a client, y'know,' Tessa assured Mel knowledgeably.

'You reckon?' Mel muttered dubiously.

'So expensively dressed, she has to be rolling in money and he would feel obliged to bring a client like her to an up-market restaurant like this for lunch, Mel.'

Fixing her mind on her delicious Dover sole, Mel reminded herself that she was enjoying a special meal, it was a lovely day and she was deliriously happy for Tessa and Josh who were such dear friends of hers. So, for how much more could a sane, sensible woman ask?

Later, raising a spoonful of raspberry mousse to her lips, she noticed Calvert walking across the room towards their table.

'What in heaven's name are you two doing here?'

A broad smile creased his face.

'We're having such a lovely time, Cal. We've been shopping for new clothes this morning, and because Mel is going back to work next Monday, she decided to make today extra special and have lunch here, although I never dreamed this place was quite so opulent.'

And while Tessa and her brother talked, Mel thought how handsome he looked today, every inch the supremely confident lawyer, but then, even as a child, she had considered him a cut above the ordinary. And she couldn't recall a time when they hadn't been good friends.

'What did you think of your lunch, Mel?'

'Definitely above average.'

She smiled back at him.

'Has your lady friend dumped you?' Tessa asked, turning from him to Melanie. 'They all do, y'know.'

'That's understandable. One can get too much of a good thing,' Melanie answered, tongue-in-cheek.

'I'll have you girls know that mine was a strictly business lunch with a very tough businesswoman who eats men like me for breakfast. But where are you going now and can I give you a lift?'

'Yes, please,' Mel was quick to reply. 'My car's parked in the multistorey and it's such a climb back to the city centre.'

'I'll take you up there. Have you left the young scallywag with Josh today, Tessa?'

'No, we're going to Grandma's to pick him up. She took him for the day.'

'Right. I'll see to the bill, then drop you off at the carpark.'

Mel shook her head.

'Leave my bill, Cal. I'm paying for lunch, thank you,' she stated firmly.

'Not while I'm here you're not,' he replied with equal firmness, his steely gaze defying her to argue.

Melanie shrugged, not prepared to raise her voice with so many people about, yet annoyed at his confidence, at him fully expecting that any woman would, without demur, go along with him and, at times, his impossibly arrogant manner.

They were leaving the restaurant when he said, 'Is there a reason for your sudden silence, Mel?'

'Your girlfriends are no doubt delighted to obey your slightest whim, Calvert Robson, but please remember I'll never be one of them.'

'What? My girlfriend? You already are and true, you're not the most accommodating one around, but I've always been prepared to overlook your faults, Mel.'

She gave him a withering look.

'Save it for your next courtroom case. They'll be more impressed.'

Tessa glanced at her friend and when

Mel saw the worried look on her face, she burst out laughing.

Quickly, Cal caught her hand, swung her into his arms and whispered, 'I'll see you later tonight.'

From their vantage point on the quayside, the scenic view of the majestic bridges spanning the sun-dappled river, the total magic of the lovely summer day as they paused on the quayside walkway, might never have existed at the precise moment she felt the pressure of his lips on her ear, creating ripples of heat to shimmy down her spine, momentarily making her oblivious of her surroundings and just about everything else.

'Come on, you two. If we don't put a spurt on, James'll be wondering where I am and Grandma's hip'll be playing her up.'

Melanie didn't utter a word, not when Cal opened his car door for her, during the short journey to the city centre carpark or when he waved them goodbye. She needed time and space, time to breathe normally and strengthen her shaky defences against Calvert's casual charm onslaughts.

That evening, he walked from the Hall to the house on Parson's Green, feeling the need to be out of doors, be alone for a while in the summer evening air. A brisk walk to Melanie's place would stretch his legs and help concentrate his mind on a few of his more pressing problems.

On impulse, he'd accepted the job Harvey Sinclair offered him, had jumped at the chance to own his own law firm despite knowing that once Mel's father retired, he was seriously going to miss his senior partner. Yet, he'd worked incredibly hard for the past five or six years, deserved the position of head of the fine, old-established law firm and once he took over the business, he could widen its scope, think of expansion, of spreading his net farther afield.

Setting up a law firm in Newcastle was beginning to look a distinct

41

possibility, and the lady he'd taken to lunch today could well be the means of furthering his plans in that direction. As he walked, Cal shrugged off his jacket, decided against a stop at the pub for a drink, knowing Mel would offer him one as soon as he called on her. Seeing her at lunchtime had been more than a mere pleasant surprise. He smiled and let the thought of their meeting linger.

She hadn't changed, not one iota. Mel, whatever the age, was Mel, the same forthright, strong, single-minded female with those big brown eyes. He'd always had to put a little pressure on her. Right from being kids, he'd had to use gentle persuasion before she'd see things his way and admit that he could, just possibly on the odd occasion, be right.

When he reached the house he saw her in the front garden busily dead-heading roses.

'What happened to Isobel Crowther's gardener?'

She looked up and smiled.

'Oh, hi, Cal. Aunt Isobel didn't have a gardener, couldn't afford one and neither can I. But Giles Shepherd has kindly loaned me a few books on the subject,' she informed him.

'You're never here long enough to tend a garden this size.'

'Or, more often than not lately, read a book,' she agreed, slipping off her gardening gloves. 'You wanted to talk to me about something,' she reminded him, turning towards the house.

'I thought that if you hadn't eaten anything since lunch, we could call at The Schooner.'

'Thanks, but I'm making myself an omelette. You're welcome to join me,' she added, quite sure he would prefer eating at the pub.

Following her into the house, he said, 'An omelette sounds perfect.'

'Help yourself to a drink. Aunt Isobel always kept a bottle of good Scotch in the dining-room sideboard for her two favourite lawyers, so my father says.'

'It's true,' he replied.

The aroma of freshly-ground coffee percolating along with the sizzle of eggs and mushrooms hitting hot butter soon made Melanie's comfortable kitchen infinitely more inviting than his original idea, Cal admitted, carrying a drink in each hand and placing one on the work surface for her. But it wasn't only the smell of food or the offer of fine old malt whisky, it was whose kitchen it was and who was preparing the meal. It was her.

'This guy, Shepherd. I was under the impression his art gallery was in London,' he began casually, placing his drink on the kitchen table and pulling out a chair.

'It is, and he lives there, but his elderly mother lives alone in King's Denton and he likes to visit her as often as he can,' she explained, wondering at Cal's sudden interest in Giles.

He relaxed, leaned back in the chair, stretched his legs and watched her, admiring the deftness of her movements.

'And visits you? Here, I'll carry those.'

Mel took a slow, deep breath.

'It'll be cooler in the sitting-room, Cal. The garden doors are open.'

Congratulating herself on having circumvented further personal questions, Mel told herself she should've known better when, halfway through the meal, he said, 'Is Giles a regular visitor?'

'He visits your sister more, and thank goodness, he'll be in Washington to help Tessa with her art exhibitions.'

He smiled.

'Sounds a nice guy. Does a lot of good works for helpless ladies, it seems.'

'I hope you're not including me in that category.'

He burst out laughing and shook his head.

'No way. Nonetheless, he has discovered your abysmal lack of gardening know-how and intends doing something to help you in that direction, but I wonder if that's all he's interested in.'

'You would, but not all men are necessarily as devious as you.'

'Oh, I don't know. With all my guile and ingenuity, I didn't get far with you. Of course, he is a lot older and could be cleverer.'

'Giles Shepherd is a charming man and a reliable, staunch friend,' she said briskly, seeing his empty dinner plate and getting to her feet.

'That's praise indeed,' he said quietly, gazing at her flushed cheeks, surprised at how quickly she had jumped to the rescue of her new friend.

'There's a bilberry tart in the oven. Can I tempt you?'

'If there's a double entendre in your question, yes, on both counts,' he replied with a wicked grin.

'With cream?' Mel replied on her way to the kitchen, unable to restrain her laughter another minute.

He had always had the capacity to make her laugh, right from their earliest childhood, and perhaps it was his overtly light-hearted nature as a young man that she found so appealing.

The attraction of opposites, Mel reflected, slicing the tart, the object of her affection appearing in the kitchen, surprising her with a loud, appreciative sniff at the steaming bilberries.

'Isn't this what you really want, Mel? And don't tell me you're not the marrying kind, or that you don't love kids. I know none of that is true.'

What next, she thought, tipping cream into a jug.

'I have an extremely demanding career, Calvert, or hadn't you noticed?'

'That's precisely what I'm talking about. Isn't it time you changed course, opted for a less dangerous job, or can't your photographer, or is it your driver . . . '

'Both happily-married men, Cal, and you should know by now that I don't play those games,' she cut in sharply, objecting to his unexpected lawyer-style delve into her personal life, yet the next moment, she was laughing at the sound of her mother's voice calling sweetly through the open letterbox, 'It's just me, Melanie.'

'I get the distinct feeling your mother isn't exactly overjoyed at the idea of you moving out of Juniper Cottage,' Cal said with a wide grin as Mel hurried to open the front door.

'I just called for a few minutes to see if you'd like to come with your father and me to the coast later in the week,' Emily began to explain, following Mel into the sitting-room, both surprised and pleased to see Calvert looking relaxed, and very much at home.

A moment later, the jangle of the phone sent Melanie into the hall again and when she walked back into the room, Cal saw at a glance that whoever her caller, judging from Mel's bemused expression, the news hadn't been at all bad.

'Would you believe that was my boss asking me if I'd stand in for one of the Newcastle newsreaders in a few weeks' time?'

'But I thought studio work was

something you'd never do.'

'On a permanent basis maybe, Cal, but don't you see, this gives me a chance to be working here prior to our trip to America, and not stuck in some outlandish place where an airport might be an unheard-of luxury. I'd hate to disappoint Tessa at the last minute.'

'Or your friend, Giles,' Cal muttered quietly.

'Well, isn't this wonderful news? We can look forward to seeing you on television every night for two weeks. You must buy some smart clothes, dear,' her mother advised, happy to think of her daughter working so near home and in a much safer environment. 'I must hurry home and tell your father. He'll be over the moon.'

Cal pushed himself out of the chair and reached for Mel's hand.

'So when d'you start this new job?'

'I'll know more after my visit to the studios tomorrow morning.'

'Then we'd better let you get your beauty sleep. Come on, Emily, I'll walk you back to Juniper Cottage.'

It was some time after they left when Mel wondered why Cal had called in the first place. She'd thought there must be a specific reason, but reckoned her mother's impromptu visit had silenced him. Then again, Calvert making an evening call was a surprise in itself, and staying for a meal even more unexpected, and not only that. He'd gone out of his way to create a warm, intimate atmosphere in her home tonight and she was at a loss to fathom his new, more than friendly demeanour.

3

Television studios were not a new venue, but working in one on a weekly basis was. It had not, even for the briefest moment, occurred to Melanie that she would enjoy the experience, but as she left the ever-present buzz of the city behind after the first exhausting week was wrapped up, she had a satisfied feeling of really having accomplished something.

The powers-that-be knew her journalistic history and had been fulsome in their praise and admiration, called her a natural and, suspecting she was nervous in their environment, had generously put themselves out to make her feel less of a stranger in their midst. And to be scrupulously honest, Mel had to admit she had thoroughly enjoyed her ground-breaking week's work at the studios.

The forecaster had said the weather would be fine and warm for the next few days and the thought of that and being back home, spending a quiet week-end in peaceful King's Denton, was what she needed most now, to relax, eat a few regular meals and get some fresh air into her lungs.

She saw the car outside as she arrived at the house and pulled up behind it, puzzled at Calvert sitting outside her door at this late hour on a Friday evening.

'To what do I owe this pleasure?' Mel called as Calvert emerged from the car with a bouquet of yellow rosebuds in his hand.

'I came to congratulate our local television star,' he said, presenting her with the flowers and bending to peck her cheek.

'Very funny, Cal,' she countered, trying her best to keep a check on her racing pulse.

'I mean every word of it. You are amazing and so professional you might've been reading the news for years, and what's more, glamorous.'

'True, I didn't wear my combat kit in the studio but don't be misled, Cal. The stuff on my face is called make-up and comes out of pots and tubes,' she replied, opening her front door. 'Want a cup of tea or something stronger? I can't offer you much to eat,' she said apologetically, turning her head and smiling up at him.

'That's really why I called. I guessed you wouldn't bring fresh food back with you and thought we could have dinner at The Schooner to celebrate your new, high-profile imagine.'

Mel thought she'd like nothing better than to have a really good meal at The Schooner with him, but shook her head.

'It's late, Cal.'

'I booked the table this morning, convinced you hadn't eaten a proper meal all week.'

'You're right there and thank you, Cal. OK, I would love to have dinner at

The Schooner,' she accepted cautiously, her mind searching for a plausible reason why he wanted a dinner date with her.

She cast a critical glance at the crumpled dress she was wearing.

'Give me a few minutes to change into something suitable.'

Twenty minutes later, Cal's eyes flicked from the top of her sleek, up-swept hair, her almost bare shoulders, down to her black, strappy sandals.

'It was well worth the wait,' he murmured appreciatively.

'And you don't look too bad yourself,' she returned the compliment in their old, bantering way.

Whilst The Schooner wasn't the only hotel in the small market town, it was undeniably the best. Beautifully appointed, the restaurant served the most outstandingly good food this side of Newcastle. No sooner were they shown to their table than Cal reminded her of the American holiday.

'How're you travelling to Heathrow?'

'Giles is picking Tessa and me up here, taking us to his London home for the night and we'll get a taxi to the airport on Monday morning.'

Surprised, Cal looked over the top from his menu at her side and said quietly, 'He's taking you to his home for the night?'

'Your sister and I. This is simply to make Tessa's journey as comfortable as possible. This is her fifth month, Cal, and I think Giles is a remarkably generous man to put himself to so much trouble.'

'Any good hotel near the airport would be comfortable, Melanie.'

'Are you implying there's an ulterior motive in his kindness? For shame, Cal. You know Giles Shepherd. He's a friend and you also know he's a really nice guy.'

'Without a single ulterior motive maybe, but not without an agenda of his own,' he replied non-committally, suddenly more interested in the food being placed before him.

Mel tasted her wine, smiled at him and said, 'Delicious.'

'That's better, you're relaxing. After the strain of being in front of those cameras all week, I'm not surprised you need to wind down. It has to be a more pleasing occupation for a journalist than being out in all weather in the bleakest places, with bombs dropping around you, bullets whizzing past your head. I'm still trying to work out why you prefer to distance yourself from us,' he said softly, his hand covering hers on the white tablecloth.

She glanced down at his strong, tanned hand.

'Having no money I have to work for a living, and I suppose it was a challenge at first. Reporting the news where it's happening is heady stuff for a journalist,' she admitted, smiling at the intensity of his gaze, recognising that he couldn't begin to understand how much she loved her job. 'I must appear rather out of the ordinary to you, Cal.'

'An enigma,' he agreed thoughtfully, interlacing his fingers through hers. 'Nonetheless a lovely, intriguing woman.'

'Hardly an enigma, Cal. You know me as well as you know Tessa.'

'Oh, I knew the girl well enough, but I was referring to you now, the woman you've become. And don't tell me those television guys aren't queuing up for your favours.'

She swallowed a forkful of fish quickly as laughter bubbled to the surface.

'Ten deep and stretching for miles,' she quipped, once her laughter subsided.

Although determined to keep her emotional distance from him, Melanie's earlier reservations about this dinner date had vanished. The food and wine were excellent, Calvert, as usual, was good company, but it was his friendly concern for her well-being she really appreciated. And for such an exceptionally busy man to show such thoughtfulness, was it any wonder she was so inordinately fond of him?

Cal looked from the waiter to her.

'Profiteroles, as usual?' he asked with a maddening grin.

'Why change the habit of a lifetime?' she responded, watching the young waiter struggle to keep his lips from twitching.

'I thought you might be on a strict new diet now you're a television star,' Cal suggested, topping up her wine glass.

'If I was, this meal has just blown my calorie count to smithereens.'

Melanie smiled, put down her wine glass and, glancing across the table, brown eyes met blue and lingered, lulling her into a false sense of trust, reminding her of the woman she had become, as Cal had called it. And this evening seemed light years away from the gauche teenager she'd been, a time when her heart could flip at the mere sight of Calvert Robson.

'You could get to like this cushy newscaster stuff, sitting in an air-conditioned studio looking perfect for the cameras. You sounded good, too, with just the right degree of warmth and a human touch that reached out to the audience. It certainly did to me and your father was visibly impressed. Said he'd no idea you were so good at your job.'

Mel laughed.

'Well, that makes two fans, but joking apart, Cal, what surprised me was their invitation to come back next week.'

'And by the sound of things you readily agreed which proves my point about the possibility of you changing your mind.'

'Being seduced by what you consider a cushy number? We'll see.'

They were on their way home after a happy, completely relaxing evening when Cal told her he would be working in London for a few days and would see little of her or Tessa before they set off for America and the Georgetown exhibition.

'I know Tessa is banking on this art show being a success and for her sake, I hope she's not setting her sights too high.'

'Don't worry about Tessa, I'll look after her. I have it all arranged. Whatever happens in Georgetown, it won't be all work. We're going to kill the two proverbial birds with a combination of Tessa's art business and as much sight-seeing as we can slot into that week.'

When he stopped the car outside the house, Mel slid him a sidelong glance.

'Would you like a coffee?'

'I'll make it and let my favourite TV personality relax in an armchair after her gruelling week,' he said, laughing at her pained expression.

While Cal was in the kitchen Melanie switched on her phone messages and her first caller had been Tessa.

'I'm getting really excited about next week. But where are you? Phone me the first minute you get. We need to talk, Mel.'

And after deciding to call on Tessa tomorrow, she then smiled broadly at hearing her mother's dulcet tones, this time a rather long message wanting to know where she was, what she was doing and to be sure to have Sunday lunch at Juniper Cottage with them, knowing how she can't have had a decent meal all the week working as she was in those television studios.

Her mum's message came as no surprise, but the next one, from Giles Shepherd, did.

'Hi, Mel. I'm home for the week and wanted to take you out for a meal, but guess you're working late. I can't wait to see you again, so what about lunch tomorrow? Phone me as soon as you get home.'

She turned to see Cal standing in the open doorway, a mug of coffee in each hand and a face like thunder.

'Ah, thanks, Cal. That was Tessa, my mum, and . . . '

'Giles, your friend who can't wait to see you again,' he cut in, placing the mugs of coffee on a nearby table. 'Well, will you?' Cal asked, crossing the room to where she stood looking puzzled by his reaction.

'Will I what?'

'Oh, come on, Mel, you must recognise his game plan. You'll have a cosy lunch together, spend the rest of the afternoon with him which he'll see as a cosy prelude to your week together in Washington.'

'And what's your game plan?' Mel countered bitterly.

'You know me better than that. Unlike me, this man is almost a stranger. You know practically nothing about Giles Shepherd.'

'You're right. I know you much better, but your cavalier attitude towards women over the last few years is hardly a recommendation for any serious-minded female to regard you in a favourable light.'

'What?'

Taken aback by the harshness of her words, he glared at her.

'How can you, of all people, think so badly of me?'

'I know you of old, Cal, and what's more, have known a number of your girlfriends, but that's not my business, just as Giles Shepherd and my relationship with him is none of yours. I have no intention of allowing you or anyone else to choose my friends. You've seriously overstepped the mark here and succeeded in making my perfectly innocent friendship with a decent man sound a cheap, tawdry affair,' she protested, trying in vain to hold back her tears.

'Good grief, Mel, don't. Please don't cry. Forgive me,' he pleaded, his arms reaching, pulling her to him. 'I don't know what's happening here, but whatever's wrong with me, you know I'd never intentionally hurt you, angel,' he told her, looking contrite, taking her wet face in his hands, his lips finding hers in a kiss that caught her breath and sent a wave of heat spiralling through her, making her want to stay in his arms and wish the moment could last for ever.

But it was the very act of wishing that made her put her hands against his chest and bring them both back to reality with a bump. Their eyes met and held for a long moment.

'Have a good time, Mel, and I'll see you when you get back, but I'll phone before you leave,' he said softly, reluctant to loosen his hold on her, his eyes searching her face. 'I should never have spoken to you in that way, Mel, I was 'way out of line. Try to forgive me.'

'Thank you for this evening, Cal. It was a lovely meal,' she began, her mind in a quandary, not sure when or how it had ended so badly.

They'd had tiffs before on all kinds of subjects, yet there had always been a bond of friendship too strong for mere argument to weaken. Tonight, for some strange, offbeat reason, their tempers had flared and they'd both said hurtful things that would take time to forgive and perhaps even longer to forget. He brushed the back of his hand across her cheek and left.

Absently, she glanced round the sitting-room wondering at his sudden, mercurial behaviour. If it had been any man other than her self-confident friend, Calvert Robson, she might've suspected him of jealousy which, in this instance, was utterly ridiculous.

What time was left of that weekend Melanie spent with her parents, guessing they were worried about the long journey to the States.

They were having Sunday lunch when her mother said, 'I met Tessa, Josh and little James in the bank yesterday, Mel. She looks so well and happy. Apparently, it's Calvert who doesn't seem himself lately.'

Instantly concerned, Mel said, 'Why? Did they say he was ill?'

'Not anything his mother could put her finger on, Tessa said, but I know Sally's worried. She says he's unusually quiet these days and she's convinced he's sickening for something.'

'He looks all right to me,' Harvey said, gazing thoughtfully at his daughter. 'Yet, I suppose he could be thinking of the extra workload he'll be taking on when I retire, but I doubt it. Cal's stronger than that.'

'He can't possibly take on all your cases as well as his own, can he?'

Her father smiled.

'He'll take on as much help as he needs, Mel. As you know, the only stipulation I've asked of Calvert Robson is that he looks after the business here in King's Denton, but it's more of a favour than a condition. You know how I trust Cal.'

It was approaching teatime when she left her parents home with promises to take care of herself, not to wear her hair pulled too severely from her face in front of the cameras next week, to have a wonderful holiday with Tessa and to phone home the minute their plane landed.

Melanie laughed quietly to herself as she strolled to Tessa's and Josh's cottage to finalise a few last details before leaving for London the following Sunday.

'Hello, Aunt Melanie,' little James called, almost falling off his bike as he tried to wave to her and negotiate a tricky curve in the garden path.

'Hi, James,' she replied, trying to undo the childproof gate fastening.

'I'll undo that for you, Mel,' Josh said, appearing at the cottage door.

'After I've cracked this, next week Fort Knox,' Mel quipped.

'If you're looking forward to your trip half as much as Tessa, you're going to have a wonderful time, Mel. She's in the kitchen baking scones for tea.'

Mel had scarcely put a foot in the kitchen when Tessa said, 'Have you seen our Calvert lately, Mel? Honestly, I don't know what's got into him, but he's snapping everybody's head off.'

'But not ill? Mother said he didn't look well and thought he might be working too hard,' Mel replied diplomatically.

'I'd be surprised if there was anything physically wrong with him. He's been working out at the gym this morning, yet when I phoned, told him you were coming to tea and asked him to come over, he said something about serious-minded females and him not wanting to put a damper on my tea party. And you know that's not like Cal at all.'

'His latest girlfriend has probably dumped him,' Mel said, feeling slightly guilty, at the same time telling herself it was high time a woman put Tessa's brother in his place.

'That's the other strange thing, Mel. There is no girlfriend and there hasn't been one for weeks. Josh thinks Cal is taking serious stock of his life, that your father's offer to head the law firm is making him think about this new, more responsible situation he suddenly finds himself facing.'

'Cal's too young for a mid-life crisis, Tessa.'

'But old enough to stop and consider the direction his life is taking.'

The following week was a long, hard slog, apart from snatching a sandwich with Giles in Newcastle at lunchtime on Tuesday.

'Your rooms in Washington are

booked and I'll arrange for a cab to pick you up and bring you and Tessa to Georgetown each morning,' he said with a smile and added, 'You'll be ready for a holiday after two weeks in your rarefied atmosphere.'

'I'm ready now,' she told him. 'It's new and exacting, but I'm finding my way around, getting acclimatised to a television studio environment which is indeed rarefied.'

Melanie had to admit, albeit to herself, that she found the work an unlooked-for challenge as well as exciting in its own, very individualistic way.

When Giles stopped his car outside the television building, he leaned across and kissed her cheek.

'Next time we eat together, it'll be a proper meal when you're not pushed for time. I'll pick you up on Sunday morning, Mel,' he promised, thinking she looked every inch the city girl today and lovelier than ever in her smart cream-coloured trouser suit.

The remainder of the week was as hectic as the beginning and feeling relief and a sense of achievement, Mel thanked her newfound studio friends for their kind help and advice, said goodbye and left the television building behind, wanting nothing more than to be out of the city and on her way home to finish off her packing.

An hour later, she was in her bedroom staring at an open suitcase, wondering how cold early September days in Washington were and if she had enough warm clothes, when the phone rang.

'If I called to wish you bon voyage would you let me through your door?' Cal enquired, waiting a moment before adding, 'Cat got your tongue, Mel?'

'When I've finished packing I'm having a bath and generally getting ready for tomorrow's trip, so yours would be a wasted journey.'

'But I could be useful, help you pack, wash your back and things.'

'Goodbye, Cal,' she said, trying not

to laugh as she slotted the phone back, telling herself there was nothing wrong with Calvert Robson, yet it was good to hear his voice, to leave for her holiday knowing they were back on speaking terms.

Ten minutes after the phone call, a loud rap at her door surprised her, but her visitor was a bigger surprise.

'Hi, Cal,' she began hesitantly, recalling his tenaciousness once he'd set his mind to do something.

He hung his head sheepishly.

'Right, you're angry, but then, so am I.'

'Well, to what do I owe the pleasure of this visit?'

'Is it your intention to keep me standing on your doorstep while you make smart remarks that are not your style?'

Pulling the door open and stepping aside to let him in, Mel figured he was in a truculent mood. Something was troubling him and she guessed letting him into her house wasn't a wise move, but she'd stay cool. Better that than causing irreparable damage to their

71

close friendship. Cautiously, they faced each other once in the sitting-room.

'I know you'll have a good time. I just wish I was going with you,' he began quietly.

'Why say that when you refused your sister's invitation to tea purely because I was at the cottage?'

'Right, with the rest of the family, when I wanted to see you alone.'

'We have so little to say these days, Cal, and when we do, it usually ends in disagreement,' she reminded him as his hand reached for hers.

'I care for you and the thought of you in the company of a man like Giles Shepherd irritates me. He's not your type,' he stated brusquely.

Controlling her temper and measuring her words, she said, 'I'm aware of your brotherly feelings, Cal, but I no longer need a minder and . . . '

Before she could utter another syllable, she was in his arms, his lips were on hers, instantaneously wiping any family relationship image clean from her mind, and so conclusively that as her world tilted, Mel was grateful for the strength and steadiness of the arms holding her.

Cal released his hold on her.

'I was right, and I've known it for years, but you're so elusive, always flying off somewhere, Mel, and you must see what's happening here.'

'If you're implying that my journalistic job has kept us apart, I find that incredibly hard to believe when each time I come home there's a new girlfriend hanging on your arm,' Mel responded, exaggerating a bit, but accurate enough to drive home the point.

'That's all in the past. I'm asking you to think about us, about you spending more time here, giving us a chance.'

'This is very sudden, Cal. You know I love what I do and travelling goes with the job. And why should I make a sacrifice like that?'

'Because I'm asking you to, but you obviously care more for your job than me,' he said, his voice hardly audible. 'This is bad timing and you need to pack, Mel. Take care of yourself.'

He took her face in his hands and his lips brushed hers.

'Remember I'm here,' he whispered.

Scarcely believing her ears, she walked slowly up the stairs, wondering what he was asking of her. Give up her job? How could she do that, and for what? Was he asking her to live with him? No. He must know she wouldn't do that and what a time to tell her that he cared, not loved her — he hadn't said that. What exactly did care encompass? It smacked of sitting on a fence to her, and he was wrong about her not caring for him. She'd done that for as long as she could remember.

4

The crowds at Heathrow on Monday morning acted like a shot of adrenalin to Melanie. She was on holiday! And whilst she'd travelled fairly widely these last few years, this was her first visit to America. She felt like a young teenager on her first flight abroad.

Glancing at Tessa deep in conversation with Giles as they waited to be called to the departure lounge, she smiled. This was a particularly exciting journey for Tessa, and Giles had been a perfect gentleman to let them stay overnight at his Fulham house. Admittedly, she hadn't slept much, but that had less to do with the strange bed than the memory of Cal's kiss and what, if anything, it meant. And plaguing thoughts had persisted about previous girlfriends he'd no doubt cared for and possibly kissed with equal fervour, and when asked to chuck their jobs for him, their various responses must've been crackers!

Mel laughed quietly to herself, at the same time wishing she wasn't such a loyal, completely dedicated admirer of that man.

When Giles picked up Tessa's bag and said, 'That's our flight they're calling, ladies,' Mel followed them to the departure lounge promising herself a holiday she not only deserved, but felt she needed. She would see something of Virginia and the sights of America's capital city. One week so unlike any other, she would put all thought of her fraught, dangerous work behind, her less than satisfactory relationship with Calvert Robson would go firmly on the back burner and she could then enjoy a week of perfect peace.

Giles grinned at her.

'You're sitting beside Tessa. You did say you'd read the book.'

Mel laughed as they boarded the plane. She had indeed read and reread the pregnancy handbook from cover to cover, knew the first few months for Tessa had been tiring, but heading for her sixth month, just as the book said, she felt her old, energetic self again. Mel gave her friend an affectionate, sidelong glance and thought she looked positively blooming.

The flight was incredibly smooth and, gazing idly out at the clear blue sky, she guessed that since the Atlantic was now behind them, it wouldn't be long before they landed. Smiling later, she gave Tessa's arm a gentle shake.

'We'll be landing soon, sleepyhead.'

'Heavens, Mel, I must've fallen asleep again.'

'And if I'd known you both snore, I would've caught the next plane,' Giles teased, laughing at the indignant look Mel turned on him.

Despite Cal's misgivings about Giles' romantic feelings for her, he'd proved such a reliable friend, she was thankful he'd decided to travel with them. Although Tessa hadn't complained, the long journey from the north-east of England must've seemed long and wearying for Tessa. Yet, Mel knew her and guessed the excitement of having her art shown in a prestigious American establishment would go a long way to keep her spirits buoyant. All they both hoped for now was a successful week.

The plane touched down smoothly and once through Customs, within minutes of Giles collecting their luggage, he escorted them out of the airport into a cab and, seeing journey's end in sight, they all gratefully sank back into the cab's comfortable seats with sighs of relief as the car sped towards Washington and their hotel.

'I'll pick you up for dinner in the rooftop restaurant later or would you prefer something lighter in the coffee shop?' Giles suggested.

Simultaneously, they refused his kind offer, neither wanting to eat, nor anything other than take a shower, make their promised phone calls home, unpack and, hopefully, catch up on some sleep.

'I can understand. Feel disorientated myself after that long haul. So, ladies, I've arranged for a cab to pick us up tomorrow morning at Sam Stern's place. He's the gallery owner in Georgetown Tessa and I've talked about, Mel. He's also a very good friend of mine.'

Mel smiled at him reassuringly.

'We're already looking forward to meeting him.'

'And don't worry, Giles,' Tessa chipped in. 'We'll be ready in good time tomorrow morning for the first day of Mr Stern's exhibition.'

The following morning, Melanie woke first, looked from her double bed to Tessa, still fast asleep in hers, swung her feet to the luxurious carpet and, inching the curtains apart, she stared in wonder, fascinated at the colourful scene that met her gaze. Dozens of presumably private little jets, business planes were either circling the sky, landing or already sitting on the Tarmac of what must be Washington's National airport.

Letting her eyes travel to the stretch of river, she saw the bridge crossing the Potomac, then directly below her what must be Army and Navy Drive, the road to the Pentagon, she assumed. She also assumed it was a fine morning, but she couldn't hear a whisper of wind or a sound of any kind. She had slept like a baby and guessed their giant-sized picture window must be quadruple-glazed!

'Good morning, Mel.'

'Great, you're awake, Tessa. Come and take a look at the view,' she said, pulling back the curtains to flood the room with sunshine.

'I can't believe the size of this bedroom. Talk about spacious. Two double beds in one room! What time is it, Mel?'

'Twenty past eight. You have the bathroom first and I'll follow.'

'What? You mean there's not two?

That's a mite stingy,' Tessa said with a giggle, joining Mel at the window. 'Wow! See what you mean. What a view, but c'mon, Mel, we'd better put our skates on or we're going to be too late for breakfast and I'm ravenously hungry.'

'I have noticed your exceptionally healthy appetite, Tessa. Are you sure you're not expecting twins?'

'No, thanks, one at a time will do nicely,' Tessa replied positively.

An hour later, Tessa and Mel were walking towards the hotel lounge when Giles met them and, at the same time, a peak-capped cab driver approached.

'Mr Shepherd, ladies,' he greeted them, his forefinger touching the peak of his cap. 'I'm Ed Donovan and Mr Stern sent me to pick you up this morning, but all you have to do anytime you want a cab this week is ring this number and I'll be here for you.'

Unbeknown to him, Ed Donovan had just taken a load off Mel's mind.

She'd been concerned about Tessa rushing about too much and getting overtired before the week was over, but Ed's offer had just solved a major part of that problem. She looked at him appreciatively and took the card from his fingers.

'Thanks, I'll pop that in my pocket.'

'Right then if we're ready, it's Mr Stern's gallery in Georgetown, Ed.'

Despite the brilliance of the sun that morning, there was an unmistakable sense of changing seasons, a gentle, but nonetheless cool reminder that summer had gone and autumn had arrived, Mel mused as they joined the traffic on the bridge spanning the Potomac.

On arriving at Samuel Stern's art gallery, Mel was pleasantly surprised, not only by the size and position of the business premises in the busy central thoroughfare, but the imposing building itself.

'Slightly more impressive than Cressy Slater's little art shop,' she whispered conspiratorially to Tessa.

Giles overheard and laughed.

'Wait till you see the inside, Mel.'

'Yeah, it's a high-class joint,' Ed joined in. 'The Washington politicians buy their pictures here and they tell me Mr Stern's a great guy to do business with.'

Mel was thinking that this was also a great place for Tessa to have her work on display. The gallery was as impressive as its elderly owner who, she reckoned, was so kind, such a warm and friendly man, that Tessa was sure to enjoy working with him. Observing her friend being introduced to various groups of potential clients, Mel could see Tessa was in her natural element, talking art, discussing her studies in England, her year in Paris, then adding a brief, though well-drawn description of her newly-built studio on the Calvert-Denton Estate.

'You were saying something earlier about going to the Smithsonian, so we can start with lunch there,' Giles suggested, suddenly appearing at Mel's elbow.

'But I thought you'd be working here all day with Sam and Tessa.'

'I'll be back in time for the early-evening session when it's sure to get busier, but at the moment, Tessa, Sam and his staff are able to cope.'

Mel looked at him thoughtfully, smiled and said, 'Yes to the lunch, and the Smithsonian. I was hoping to see everything.'

'I'd say that's impossible in little more than a week, but we'll make a start with the Air and Space museum after lunch.'

And that was the beginning of after-noons Mel and Giles spent together, either visiting museums and galleries or following the tourist route with trips to The White House, Mount Vernon and the eye-stretching Skyline Drive. Melanie had a wonderful time. Giles had been to both Washington DC and New York many times and proved to be a fund of knowl-edge on all things American, and although they parted company shortly after tea each day, she enjoyed the carefree, holiday atmosphere of their afternoon forays along the tourist trail and it was plain to see that Giles was also having a really good time.

On the other hand, Tessa's week had been an extraordinarily busy one, a typically nose-to-the-grindstone seven days. Yet, by the end of her sojourn at the Georgetown Art Gallery, to her utter astonishment and absolute delight, every single one of her paintings had been sold.

'Snapped up,' Tessa said jubilantly to Mel at dinner on the last night of their visit. 'I still can't believe how successful this venture has been and without doubt the most illuminating week of my entire life, from any standpoint, incredibly fulfilling and so rewarding. Even Sam Stern is stunned that things have broken all previous records, this being the most successful exhibition of his thirty years in the trade, he told Giles this evening. What a lucky break for me, Mel.'

'I'm so happy for you, Tessa, and luck might play a part, but you're a talented lady and deserve this special recognition.'

'And I can't begin to thank you for being here for me, Mel.'

'I've had a wonderful time, thoroughly enjoyed a magically, peaceful week, eating regular meals for a change, seeing some of the most jawdropping sights every day and sleeping in a warm, comfortable bed at night. My idea of heaven, Tessa.'

'The thing is, you've been here, my back-up team, always on call if I needed you and that's meant a lot to me. And just think, Mel, when all those loose ends have been tied up at the gallery tomorrow, we'll be on our way home.'

'And no matter how good the holiday, it's always good to return home,' Mel said with a sigh — and Calvert Robson immediately and annoyingly came to mind!

'Do you have to go into Georgetown tomorrow? I think it's time you slowed down, started to take things easy,' she asked her friend.

'The thing is, I promised Sam I'd call tomorrow morning. I saw how tired he looked when I left him tonight and he has been so kind and helpful to me, I hadn't the heart to leave him and Giles to tackle a mountain of work that's still waiting to be cleared up.'

Mel smiled at Tessa's wistful expression.

'I suspect you're beginning to miss Josh and Jamie.'

'That has to be an understatement.'

'And after your incredible success this week, we should be drinking champagne tonight, but for your condition. Still, I'm not complaining. I can't recall a better holiday, certainly not one where I've never given work a thought for a moment, or done anything more strenuous than eat and sleep,' Mel said light-heartedly, raising her glass of Californian wine to toast her friend's achievement.

Tessa glanced impishly across the table.

'And perhaps our mutual friend has something to do with this happiest of holidays? I know Giles has enjoyed your company enormously this week. Could he be hoping for more than your friendship? And why isn't he having his dinner with us this evening?'

'He's having his farewell meal in Georgetown with Sam, and with that incorrigible romantic streak of yours, Tessa Maitland, you're beginning to sound just like my matchmaking mother!' Mel laughed.

'But your mother has her hopes set on Calvert and you getting together, and unlike Giles, my dear brother is showing no sign of being serious with any female. There isn't even a casual girlfriend to be seen these days, not for ages. He seems to be taking life much more seriously than ever before.'

'That could be the extra responsibility he's taking on with the Newcastle venture, and from the little my father has told me about Cal's plans, it sounds a backbreaking workload,' Mel said, thinking of his ironic accusation that she was never there, always traipsing off to some remote part of the world and was it any wonder they couldn't spend more time together.

'Oh, Mel, won't it be good to be home, see them all again?'

Glancing across the table at her vulnerable friend, Mel gave a sympathetic nod.

'I'll come to the art gallery with you and Giles tomorrow morning. You might need an extra pair of hands. But your finishing-off work notwithstanding, we must get back from Georgetown and be at the airport in good time for our plane.'

'You know what an organised guy Giles is, Mel. With him around there's not the remotest chance of us missing our flight home. I know he has already booked Ed's taxi to take us to the airport.'

'And while we're on the subject of playing safe, you should have an early night, Tessa. For a lady six months pregnant, you've had a fairly hectic schedule. I just hope you're not overdoing things.'

'This week has been great fun for me. I wouldn't have missed the buzz and excitement of having my pictures shown here, not for anything. And don't worry, I feel fit.'

It was very early the following morning when Mel opened her eyes. Her first thought was of Cal, of being back in King's Denton and seeing him again, musing on the possibility that Tessa was right, he was thinking seriously about his personal life and so, might it not follow that his last loving embrace and heart-stopping kiss had meant something more to him than she'd dare believe?

Silently chiding, calling herself a fool to go down that road again, she swung her legs out of bed as the phone buzzed.

'Good, it's you, Mel. How about coming with Tessa and me to George-town for an hour or so this morning?

I've a few unsold pictures from my London gallery to pack and there's some general straightening up to do before we head for the airport.'

'I'd love to, Giles, although I was looking forward to a dip in the Potomac before I left Washington DC behind,' she replied with a chuckle, glancing across the bedroom at Tessa's struggle to drag herself out of a deep sleep.

'Save it for the coaly Tyne, when we can have fun together. But seriously, we should be down for breakfast in half an hour. Ed will be outside waiting for us with his engine running at eight sharp.'

As Mel put the phone down, a mumbled, almost smothered voice asked, 'Who is that phoning in the middle of the night?'

'Giles reminding us that we're going home today and if we want breakfast this morning, you'd better make a move.'

'What d'you mean, if we want breakfast — I'm starving,' she mumbled sleepily, before attempting to sit up, yawning inelegantly, her blonde hair a tousled mop, her eyes struggling to focus.

Fortunately, Mel hadn't envisaged their trip to the art gallery that morning would be a walk in the park. She saw the amount of packing and general work to be done as soon as she arrived at the gallery, and all to be completed in the short time they had before their flight. The other fortunate thing was that Sam Stern was waiting for them, making four pairs of willing hands in all, she thought gratefully.

Mel was allocated the task of stacking a series of small watercolours, all coastal scenes. Giles was up a ladder, unhooking a few of his paintings displayed high on the gallery walls, passing them down to Sam and Tessa who were carefully wrapping, crating and marking them for their return journey to London.

They were a good team, an efficient working machine, Mel mused, glancing at Giles as he moved the tall ladders across the gallery floor to climb up again and stretch, this time reaching to unhook a large, gilt-framed oil painting. She held her breath, stared as though momentarily transfixed, watching the ladder move and tilt.

'Out of the way!' Giles shouted.

The ladder fell to the floor, sending Giles crashing, his fall broken by a large, heavy oak table. Mel heard Tessa scream, and turning, looked down at Giles, saw his twisted foot, blood trickling from his forehead, then looking up, saw Sam's shocked face.

'We need an ambulance, Sam,' she said quietly.

'Yes, Mel. He needs more help than we can give him. I'll get in touch with the hospital right away.'

She saw Tessa looked pale and was instantly concerned.

'He hit his head, knocked himself out and might have twisted an ankle, but a doctor will soon fix all that,' Mel said in a calming tone, kneeling at the side of their friend and taking his hand in hers.

'So perhaps he's not too badly hurt. D'you think we should bathe the blood off his face?'

Mel looked at her watch. The only sure thing on her mind at that precise moment was how to get Tessa on the plane leaving for Heathrow in little over an hour while she accompanied Giles to the hospital and discover just how seriously hurt he was. Yet how could she leave Tessa to make that long journey back home alone?

'We'd better leave everything to the paramedics. They'll know best,' Mel replied, wishing either her mother or Tessa's was here in her place, both ex-nursing sisters with years of experience.

'Ambulance is on its way,' Sam stated, walking back into the room. 'And you two ladies have a plane to catch, so I'll get Ed to pick up your luggage from the hotel and get you to the airport in time. And try not worry about Giles. I'll look after him.'

'Thanks, Sam, but I can't go along with that. I don't want to leave Giles until I know more about his injuries, but after promising her family to be at Tessa's side during this trip and get her home safely, I'm loath to let her take the long journey home alone.'

The sound of the ambulance arriving brought their conversation to an abrupt halt and the anxious trio watched as two paramedics, with the utmost care and obvious skill, slowly eased Giles on to a stretcher, then quickly carried him from the gallery to the waiting ambulance.

'You go with him, Mel. I'll bring Tessa in my car.'

The décor of the hospital waiting-room was light and airy, but Mel's thoughts were far from appreciating the beauty of either the hospital's architecture or pleasant décor. Giles and if he'd regained consciousness was her uppermost concern. Bones could be mended she reasoned, but his head had taken a bad knock and would need to be scanned before they knew the extent of the damage.

Deep in thought, she heard Tessa's voice and forced a smile.

'Come and sit in this comfortable chair beside me, Tessa.'

'Sam's parking the car. He phoned the airport desk from the gallery and explained everything. He also insists we stay with him at his home until we know more about Giles. Have you been told anything yet?'

'These things take time. And you'll have to phone Josh soon. He's going to be very disappointed and worried about you, I imagine.'

'So will James, but in that instance, disappointment is putting it mildly. Look, Mel, the approaching white coat could be Giles' doctor.'

The man was slim, rangy, Mel thought as she stood, then took a few steps towards him, effectively blocking his path.

'Excuse me. Can you tell me anything about Giles Shepherd, if he has regained consciousness?'

'Are you his wife?'

'No. This is Mrs Maitland, Mr Stern and I'm Melanie Sinclair. We're friends and were working with him when the accident occurred.'

'I see. Well, your friend's a very lucky man not to be badly concussed after such a blow on the head, and although he's fully conscious again, we must keep him under observation a little longer.'

Sighing with relief and resignation in equal parts, Mel managed a smile.

'We were booked on a flight for England today.'

'I'm afraid Mr Shepherd's not fit to travel anywhere today or tomorrow. The head injury apart, when he fell, he sustained a fracture to his right ankle, so he'll be hobbling for quite some time.'

'Poor Giles,' Tessa commiserated. 'How soon can we see him?'

'He must rest now, but should be out of pain and feeling a lot better by tomorrow afternoon.'

She glanced up at the doctor, thinking his eyes looked too big for his unusually slim face, yet so kind, gentle, like his quietly reassuring voice.

'We'll come back tomorrow. And thank you, Doctor. It's a great relief to know my friend will soon be on the mend. I was afraid his injuries might be much worse.'

Sam shook the doctor's hand.

'Anything he needs, don't spare the expense. I'll see to all that.'

And while the girls regretted missing their flight home, they left the hospital feeling nothing but a profound sense of gratitude that the news was better than they'd dared hope.

'Come on, get in the car. I'm taking you girls straight to my home to make the necessary phone calls home before your families get a chance to worry about you.'

'Are you sure we won't be too much trouble, Sam?'

'Trouble? Having two pretty girls in my home? I'm an old dyed-in-the-wool bachelor, Tessa, with a housekeeper old enough to be my mother, so having you young things living in the house for a few days'll be a rare treat for me.'

And if Mel had been impressed with Sam's business premises, when the car pulled up in a Georgetown crescent of large, imposing terrace houses, she smiled, recalling their taxi driver's comment about Mr Stern's flourishing business and how old man Stern must be loaded!

Half an hour later, Mel was standing in a large, comfortably-furnished room gazing out of a window at a well-tended garden, while Tessa was on the phone, telling Josh about their unavoidable delay, explaining that they'd be here for another two or three days, because Mel wouldn't let her travel home alone. Smiling, Mel turned from the window to Tessa who was holding out the phone to her.

'There's a guy on the line wants to talk to you, Mel.'

When she heard the familiar sound of Cal's voice ask quietly, 'How are you coping, Melanie?' she felt a tight little knot and could neither speak nor stem the tears that sprang to her eyes. She cleared her throat.

'We're fine, Cal,' she managed to murmur.

'I'm sorry about Giles, sounds a nasty accident. Look, angel, after you've been to the hospital tomorrow, you should have more news, so phone me at the office. And, Mel, thanks for keeping Tessa under your wing. I always could rely on you.'

Following the housekeeper to a bedroom later, she saw her luggage had arrived from the hotel and blessed Sam Stern, a man rather like herself, the reliable type. She sat on the bed with its pretty patchwork quilt, and wondered about Cal Robson who always could rely on her. She asked herself why, if he admired reliability, had he chosen a succession of clinging, fly-by-night females for girlfriends? And if, as her father had tried to assure her, it meant nothing more than Cal having a youthful fling, why had it ended so abruptly?

While Tessa's phone call to Josh had been calm, almost businesslike, surprisingly so, the moment she heard Cal's voice, she had reacted like an emotional juvenile. But then his voice reminded her of home and the strange thing was, she longed to be there, wanted to get Tessa safely back to her husband in King's Denton before her baby decided to surprise them with a spectacularly early arrival.

Yet Tessa remained cool despite the trauma of Giles' accident, and she had always regarded Mel the strong one! Mel gave a short laugh and went in search of her unfazed friend.

'Isn't this the prettiest bedroom, Mel?'

'Brilliant. It's a beautiful house and I'm exceptionally grateful to Sam for rescuing us, you particularly. And after his initial disappointment, Josh will feel the same, I'm sure.'

'Heavens, Mel, it's not a big deal. We're here for an extra couple of days and the shops here are fabulous. I thought it would be fun to go shopping tomorrow, buy something nice for Giles, have lunch in Georgetown then call at the hospital to see him.'

She looked vulnerable, Mel conceded with a broad smile, but every now and then Tessa's indomitable spirit surfaced to prove the old adage about looks being deceptive.

And Tessa was right. The shops in the Georgetown Mall were wonderfully attractive and they decided to buy Sam Stern a thank-you present, and Giles a collection of magazines and books.

'Look, when we get to the hospital, would you like to spend some time alone with Giles? He does like you a lot, Mel.'

The feeling was mutual. She liked his easy-going, charming manner and Giles was someone she owed a debt of gratitude for his kindness to her during their stay in Washington. She took the bag of weighty magazines out of Tessa's hand and looked at her watch.

'Time for lunch, and no, Giles and I

don't want to be alone. Anyway, your incessant chatter will take his mind off his aches and pains.'

After lunch, Mel had to agree. Tessa's idea of spending the day was not only diverting, but a welcome morale booster, and on arriving at the hospital, a further boost to their spirits was seeing Giles sitting in a chair talking to a pretty nurse, looking so well, Mel couldn't believe his rapid recovery.

'What a lovely surprise,' he greeted them, 'and what a crass idiot you must think me. That fall must've been frightening for you, Mel.'

'Small wonder with you knocked out cold,' Tessa replied dramatically.

'Sam told me how you ladies flatly refused to board that plane and go home without me and I can only thank you both and say I've never known such kindness or generosity.'

Mel stared at him, deeply touched.

'So, yesterday was bad news, but Tessa and I were hoping for some good news today.'

Realistically, Mel thought his early release from hospital unlikely, judging by his bandaged head, his entire foot encased in plaster and the rest of his body no doubt feeling the bruising after-effect of that heavy fall.

'Can you walk, I mean, put your weight on that foot at all, Giles?'

'I'd better be able to, Tessa, or we'll miss tomorrow's plane home.'

'Are you sure you'll feel well enough to travel so soon?'

Mel's surprise was evident in her disbelieving voice.

'My doctor thinks I might as well be sitting comfortably on a plane as in his hospital all day, and Sam phoned earlier to say everything had been fixed for the flight home tomorrow. You'll be anxious to get back to King's Denton again, Tessa.'

'I will, and must phone Josh right away.'

'And I must get in touch with Mum and Dad,' Mel added, happy for Giles yet inexplicably happier at the thought of going home tomorrow.

5

'We're home,' Tessa burst out jubilantly, grasping Mel's arm as the plane touched down smoothly at Heathrow.

'Home,' Mel repeated on a sigh, every bit as happy as Tessa to be back, her thoughts on seeing her mum and dad again, and then there was Calvert and being back in King's Denton in her house on the green.

Patting Tessa's hand, she turned to Giles.

'How are you feeling?'

'Great, Mel. It's good to be back in London.'

They were almost out of the airport when, momentarily, Mel fancied her eyes were playing tricks on her, yet it certainly looked like him. Tessa pointed a finger in his direction.

'Look, it's Cal!' she shouted.

Of course it was. How could she

mistake him for any other man, Mel asked herself, searching for a logical reason for him waiting here and looking good enough to make a girl's heart skip a beat. The glaringly obvious answer, she decided, had to be his eagerness to see Tessa safely back home with her family

Giles looked distinctly puzzled.

'Did you arrange for Cal to meet you and take you back to King's Denton?'

Mel shook her head.

'It's a complete surprise to me. He has probably been working in London today and Josh would give him our flight number and time of arrival. To be honest, I'd like to get Tessa back home as quickly as possible and only hope he has come for that purpose.'

'Oh, Cal. It's so good of you to come.'

'How are you, Tessa?'

He wrapped his arms around his sister in a bear hug, his eyes moving to Melanie's face.

'You have come to take us home?'

'I have, Tessa. But how about you?' he asked, gazing steadily at Mel.

'I had a wonderful holiday, thanks, except for the accident,' she replied, turning to Giles with a warm smile.

When the two men shook hands, Cal looked at him sympathetically.

'We were all sorry to hear about your accident. What rotten luck. But look, Giles, we'll get you home first before we do anything.'

'I'll get a cab, thanks. My journey's a lot shorter than yours and the girls are feeling shattered after the shock of my fall.'

'You will take care, Giles,' Mel entreated.

'I will, and I'll phone you soon. Have a safe journey.'

Glancing from one to the other, Cal suspected that however close their friendship before, the week they'd spent in each other's company appeared to have done no harm at all to their cosy relationship. And if seeing Cal at the airport was a surprise, the sheer size and luxury of the unfamiliar car he had waiting for them was another for Mel.

'There are cushions and a blanket in the back for you, Tessa, and plenty of room to put your feet up. Come in front with me, Mel. You can keep me from falling asleep on the way back.'

'New car? Looks sumptuous and frighteningly powerful, but it's a long drive home and if you can force yourself to trust a mere female, I can always take the wheel for a spell.'

'What you can do is tell me all about your holiday, the wonderful places you visited and the exciting adventures you had with Giles. That should both satisfy my curiosity and keep me from nodding off.'

Melanie fastened her seat belt and eyed Cal narrowly.

'If you're looking for a kiss-and-tell story, you'll be disappointed,' she replied in a similarly bantering tone.

Nonetheless, while Tessa slept, Mel did talk about Samuel Stern and his kindness to them, his art gallery and some of the sights she'd seen.

'Some of the most breathtaking scenery, Cal, like the range upon range of snow-capped mountain tops we saw from one of the incredibly high vantage points on Skyline Drive.'

'With Giles, of course.'

'And I loved the botanical gardens and would liked to have seen more of them, but we never seemed to have enough time.'

'I can imagine how much Giles would appreciate the famous gardens.'

Despite trying to ignore his unsubtle remarks, Mel had to smile.

'I did warn you, Mel, he's a smooth operator.'

'Perhaps we shouldn't judge people by our own low standards, Cal, and for goodness' sake, don't talk so loudly or you'll wake Tessa.'

Speeding north on the motorway, they soon left Leeds behind and with a sidelong glance, Mel guessed he was tired.

'We should stop, if only to stretch

your legs, or let me drive for a while and give you a short break.'

'There's very little traffic on the road and Tessa's still sleeping. I'll stop at the next service station and get you a cup of tea. And I could get used to the idea of you caring about me,' he added softly.

Feeling too travel weary to comment, even think of anything other than the seductive comfort of the luxurious new car, Mel closed her eyes and felt herself drifting. It was the touch of Cal's hand on her cheek that woke her.

'Where am I?' she murmured sleepily.

'You're home, Mel.'

She looked at Cal anxiously.

'Tessa? Is she all right?'

'She's at Briar Rose Cottage with Josh and I expect fast asleep in her bed by now and that's where you should be, in your bed.'

'I must've been asleep for hours. I know I've never been so tired.'

'Completely exhausted, I'd say, but

we'll soon fix that,' he assured her, picking up her suitcases. 'Open the door and then straight to bed.'

He didn't need to tell her twice. Half asleep, she stumbled into the bedroom where she peeled off her clothes, pulled on a nightdress and slipped blissfully between cool cotton sheets.

'Would you like that cup of tea I promised you hours ago?'

Surprised to see Cal standing at her bedroom door looking almost asleep on his feet, she said, 'You should be in bed, Cal.'

'Yeah, I'm on my way,' he muttered, coming into the room, sitting on the edge of her bed and taking her hand in his.

She guessed he was just about too tired to move another inch.

'The bed's made up in the back bedroom,' she suggested tentatively.

'Thanks, angel, but I have my eye on one where I'd wake up in the morning with you in my arms looking as you do now, your hair ruffled, rosy-cheeked and edible. But you don't have to remind me. I know an overnight stay here would compromise you and anyway, you know how scared I am of your mother. So sleep tight, love,' he said softly, his lips brushing hers.

Mel laid her head on the pillow, the thud of the front door being pulled shut the last sound she heard before falling into a deep sleep.

As brilliant sunshine flooded her bedroom, Mel's eyes were forced open to focus on her mother standing at the foot of her bed.

'Good. You've had a nice, long sleep, Melanie. Calvert asked me to leave it as late as I could before letting myself in.'

Not yet fully awake, Mel propped herself up, summoned a smile as she gazed at her mum, thinking she hadn't changed one iota over the years. If anything, she looked younger than ever, still slim, smartly dressed.

'Good morning, Mum. It's good to be back home.'

'Your father and I were sorry to hear

about Giles. What a dreadful accident to have so far away from home. And you also had Tessa on your hands. It can't have been much of a holiday for you, pet.'

'Well, we're safely back and Giles Shepherd's injuries aren't as bad as they might've been. The hospital doctor thought him a very lucky man.'

'You really like Giles, don't you, Mel?'

Mel swung her legs out of the bed.

'He's a good friend, Mum, that's all,' she replied with a smile, alive to the subtleties of her mother's probing where marriage, to her, was always a possibility, however tenuous the relationship.

'He's such a nice man,' Emily Sinclair said with a tender glance at her daughter. 'I brought some fresh bread, milk and other stuff, so if you're getting up now, I'll pop downstairs and see to breakfast.'

Standing at her bedroom window, her eyes scanned the village green, the white cricket pavilion and beyond, The Dog and Duck, her father's favourite pub. The restful scene brought to mind her Aunt Isobel, and made her ponder again and on her aunt's reason for leaving this house to her.

She had been a shrewd woman, and they had always been good friends, the type of other woman a young girl could confide in. Nevertheless, her gift of this house to a single young woman who spent the best part of her life away from King's Denton, had raised a few eyebrows. A woman of hard-headed practicality would have a solid reason for leaving the home she loved to her, and Mel suspected that astute lady had sensed her growing disenchantment with her precarious lifestyle.

The smell of sizzling bacon drifted to her, a pungent reminder of when she'd last eaten. Hurriedly, she pulled on a pair of old jeans, T-shirt and trainers, then joined her mother in the kitchen.

'That smells good, Mum. And wasn't it incredibly good of Cal to call at the airport to pick us up, and dead lucky for us that he was working in London yesterday.'

'Working in London? But he wasn't. Cal wasn't working anywhere near London yesterday, Melanie. They were in the office when your father happened to mention the arrival time of your plane and Cal decided there and then to go and pick up you and Tessa. Your father told me he contacted a friend and borrowed his bigger, more comfortable car and shot off to Heathrow. And my goodness, we were proud of you for staying with Giles after his accident, but I worried that being so far from home, you'd taken too much upon yourself with the possibility of Tessa going into labour and then Giles lying on the gallery floor concussed, with broken bones and goodness only knew what else.'

Mel glanced at her plate of bacon and eggs, picked up her knife and fork and understood. Her mother was such a worrier.

'And you can imagine how poor Josh felt having to constantly placate little James who wouldn't be consoled, pestering his daddy for hours on end wanting to know when his mummy would be home.'

'Poor Josh. But we had a lovely time, despite that last-minute, unforeseen hitch. And the doctor assured us that the cut on Giles' head and the fractured bone in his foot were straightforward injuries, that apart from needing time to heal, he didn't envisage any complications, but I'll ring Giles this afternoon to see how he is.'

'And it would be nice if you called at the office to see your dad today. That would put a smile on his face. You know he's every bit as twitchy as I am when it's time for you to set off on one of your assignments.'

'I'm going to the bank, so I'll call and see him on the way,' Mel said, busily spreading marmalade on a slice of toast when she heard the car.

'It's Calvert, Mel. How strange for him to call at this time of day.'

Cal followed Mel into the kitchen and gave Emily's cheek a peck.

'She looks a lot better than she did last night before I chased her into bed,' he said with a conspiratorial wink at Mel.

Mel gave him a withering look.

'She's the cat's mother, Calvert Robson. He was referring to seeing me home, Mum.'

'And tucking you into bed, don't forget.'

'Yes, er . . . well, I'm sorry Cal, dear, but I must get back to Juniper Cottage and get Harvey's lunch or he'll be wondering what has become of me.'

Fuming, but holding her temper on a tight rein, Mel saw her mother to the front door.

'See you and Dad later,' she said, watching her walk away, no doubt now worrying about her daughter becoming just another of Cal's many female, casual girlfriends.

Slamming the front door shut, she turned on him.

'You are, without exception, the most embarrassingly insensitive man I have ever met,' she exploded. 'What's my mother to make of a remark like that? And much worse, what will my poor father think?'

'Calm down, Mel. It's time they knew what's happening here.'

'Nothing's happening here, not between you and me. And it's time you realised that I'll never be just another of your girlfriends,' Mel snapped, glaring at him, incensed to see that he was actually smiling at her.

'You could never be just another anything. You're too special.'

'You can't expect me to fall for a line like that. And while I'm grateful for the lift home from the airport, let's get something clear, Cal, once and for all. You know I'm not your type and that I don't play frivolous games with people's emotions,' she told him solemnly.

When he reached for her hand, his

face was no longer smiling and his voice harsh.

'I have never before told a woman she was special to me, nor do I play with their emotions. And lately, I could've sworn there was more between us than mere friendship. I know my feelings for you go much deeper, Mel.'

Her anger vanished as quickly as it had flared, his last few words taking her breath away, and leaving them staring at each other. Cal ran the back of his hand across her cheek.

'Sure, I've known a few girls, but nothing serious, not with any one of them, Mel, believe me.'

'Look, let's forget this conversation, Cal. And there's no need to justify your past relationships to me.'

'And where does Giles Shepherd come into this? His intentions are patently obvious, but what about your feelings for him? That's all I'm concerned about.'

Mel didn't know what to make of his visit this morning and was she expected to believe his little speech? She couldn't trust herself to take him seriously, believed his feelings for her went no further than a caring concern about a possible future relationship with a man Cal regarded as a stranger in their midst. She glanced up at him.

'I'm sorry, Cal, can't seem to get my act together today, not thinking straight and reckon it must be jet lag.'

Her voice dropped to barely a notch above a whisper.

'Not even sure about my job anymore.'

Cal looked bewildered.

'What's the matter? Are you ill? Your job's the one thing you've never had a single doubt about. What are you saying, Mel? You'd give up your job for Giles, move to London and live with a man you hardly know?'

'It has taken me ten years to build my career in journalism and I can't see myself throwing it all away, but what's abundantly clear are the very difficult decisions I need to make.'

Cal realised there was a lot more troubling her than a romantic attachment to a London art dealer.

'And are you going to tell me what has brought this to the surface?'

'An accumulation of things, like living permanently out of travel bags, feeling rootless and, for the first time, wanting to stay put in a home of my own. I'm beginning to think that my work, one mission to some distant country after another, has lost its attraction for me.'

'Now, Mel, that really has to be jet lag talking.'

'Know a good psychoanalyst?'

'I know you don't need one. Have you spoken to your boss about the way you feel?'

'Not yet. I will soon, but at the moment I'm just happy to be home.'

Cal would've preferred it if she'd added, 'And be with you again, so why don't we forget about everything but us and do something about the way we feel for each other?'

He watched her eyes fill with tears and drew her gently into his arms, held her head against his chest, breathing in the soft, subtle scent of her, feeling her warmth and softness, but this wasn't the kind of advantage he wanted, not an unfair one, not with Melanie Sinclair.

'They say fresh air's good for jet lag, Mel. Got any plans for today?'

She eased herself out of his arms.

'Sorry about the tears and, yes, I desperately need some money from the bank and I thought I'd call at the office and see Dad, but don't worry, Cal. I promise not to upset your staff with another blubbing session.'

'You used to like working for the local newspaper, so you might consider working from home, writing for one of the national daily papers. When you phone your boss to tell him you're looking for a change, why don't you sound him out about that newscaster's job you did before going to Washington?'

'On that occasion I was standing in

for someone who was temporarily away. I doubt if there'll be a vacancy to apply for. Television is a hugely competitive medium.'

'Maybe, but you were so professional, looked so good, too, and with your journalistic experience, there has to be a chance for you.'

'Thanks for the vote of confidence, but just looking good doesn't hold much sway in that highly-competitive industry. The environment is more aggressive than you think, Cal, full of people out to make their mark, plus a huge dollop of luck to fall their way.'

'But you would be interested in a job like that? You'd ask him?'

She acknowledged his persistence with a smile and a nod.

'I'll ask to meet him and we'll talk.'

'Good. See you in the office later.'

Cal sat in the car brooding. He fastened his seat belt, wondering what was troubling her. Jet lag or disenchant-ment with her career apart, she had something on her mind and it wouldn't surprise him to learn that Giles Shepherd had wasted no time, had possibly asked her to marry him. Still, Melanie Sinclair wouldn't be overly impressed with the trappings of his obvious success in the art world. Then again, Giles was the smooth, more mature and supremely confident type that attracted women.

Cal started the engine thinking of how, at times, she looked so fragile, yet he'd never met a stronger-willed or more infuriatingly independent female in his life. And she was right, there had been other girls, but he couldn't recall any one of them being half as pretty, as interesting, or as disturbing as Mel.

His lips curled in a wry smile. How could he have been so slow to see that the grass was greener nearer home? And while feeling better for seeing her, his visit had done nothing to change her mind and finally dispel the doubts she still had about his trustworthiness. That was the problem. She didn't entirely trust him and he could hardly blame her, so there was some serious bridge-building ahead. Yet, there were times when she looked at him, when he could've sworn she cared more than she was prepared to open her mind or her heart to.

He stopped the car outside the Sinclair & Robson offices in the High Street feeling despondent, wondering if he was already too late, blaming himself for not speaking up sooner, telling her exactly how he felt before she left for the States.

An hour later and feeling much calmer, Cal heard Harvey Sinclair greet his daughter and smiled, told himself he hadn't slammed doors behind him or, come to that, felt so inadequate since he was a kid. Still, in this instance there were mitigating circumstances. He'd never been in love before.

6

Harvey Sinclair listened to his daughter and when she was finished he stared disbelievingly at her for a long moment.

'Well, I'll be . . . ' he began.

'I knew you'd be surprised, but this is not a whim, Dad. I've given long and serious thought to it, from every possible angle. After ten years, I'm hanging up my combat boots or whatever the appropriate expression is.'

She smiled, happy to see her father again.

'I'm not just surprised, I'm stunned, but it's the best news I've heard in many a long day,' Harvey said, beaming back at her. 'Your mother will sleep more peacefully when you break this news to her. So you're retiring early, before your father, pet. That's a novel idea!'

'Calvert thought I ought to try the

local television news again, this time on a permanent basis, but they're inundated with clever, good-looking women looking for what's generally regarded as one of the plum, glamorous jobs.'

Mel glanced towards the door when Cal strode in, slapped a brown folder on Harvey's desk and said, 'You'll need that for the Jones' case tomorrow morning,' and turning to Mel with a smile, he added, 'Hi again, sweetheart.'

'I've spoken to the rest of the team about my decision. You've met Ed and Pete, Dad, and strangely, they instantly understood my reaction, had apparently thought my workload too heavy over the past year or two and, like you, Cal, they suggested I tried for the cushier, local television news.'

'And what happened when you phoned your superior? Fell off his corporate chair, did he? And when you asked him for the television presenter's job, after your boss picked himself up off the floor, what did he say?' Cal persisted.

'Calvert, you're incorrigible. An attitude like that would put any employer off. But if you're really interested, he did invite me to meet him in Newcastle for lunch next Friday. But now you must excuse me. I promised Tessa I'd call at the studio and have tea with her.'

'My car's outside, I'll take you over.'

When they left the office, Mel opened Cal's car door.

'I hate the idea of dragging you away from your work. I felt like walking and could easily have strolled through town to the estate.'

'I know how independent you can be, Mel. I wish sometimes you were not quite so single-minded. Even your father thinks it's time someone took you in hand.'

'And, of course, you agreed.'

'No, Mel. What you need is someone to care for you,' he said softly, stopping the car outside the estate lodge.

'Now, on such a lovely day, this is the perfect place for a walk,' she said, switching the conversation to safer, less personal ground.

Cal could see she had things on her mind.

'Great idea. Fancy a quiet stroll? Come on then. I'll show you the new stepping stones I've laid across the river beyond the five oaks.'

Mel laughed.

'What? So you can push me in again? Grow up, Robson!'

He grabbed her hand.

'I was eight years old, Mel, you were wobbly and I extended a helping hand,' he tried to explain, and laughed with her.

Looking about her, Mel thought the estate looked beautiful. Luckily, while cold, it was dry today and in the clear blue sky, a lukewarm sun offered a token warmth. She shivered and pulled her coat collar higher up her neck.

'Did you really put these stones in the river yourself?'

'Every single one of them, chose each one individually and fetched them from the quarry in the estate truck. You sound surprised,' Cal replied, swiftly retrieving her hands as they sauntered towards the five oaks.

'You always struck me as being too busy with your legal work to bother much with estate matters.'

'I don't have to do any work on the estate myself, but it is my home, Mel, and every now and then, when I crave a few hours' fresh air, I can usually find a manual job that needs doing.'

Mel looked up at him and smiled. Cal thought it would be so easy now, this minute, to tell her what was on his mind, but he held back, unsure of his ground, needing to know more about her feelings. He raised her hand to his lips, more ambivalent about telling Mel that he loved her than he would ever have believed possible.

'For a largely desk-bound lawyer, I'm all admiration,' Mel remarked thoughtfully, observing the wet stepping-stones glistening in the sunlight.

'Talking of desk-bound lawyers, Mel, I've been looking at office property in

Newcastle recently with a view to opening a Sinclair & Robson branch there and expanding the business.'

It took a minute or two for Mel to digest this momentous piece of news.

'I'd no idea. Have you been successful?'

That Calvert was ambitious she had always known, and might have expected he would eventually seek bigger offices, perhaps employ more help when her father bowed out, but somewhere in or near King's Denton. Never for a moment had it occurred to her that his sights were set farther afield, certainly not on Newcastle.

'It'll take some time to settle, a couple of months at least, but it's in hand, and your father agrees that Newcastle's the place for it.'

'You've obviously been working on this for some time, yet haven't mentioned it before today,' she reminded him.

'That could be because it's so difficult to catch you these days. Is that really going to change now, or when you meet your boss on Friday, will he talk you into taking on another assignment with your favourite driver and photo-journalist?'

'There's not a chance of that happening. I promise you that whatever move I make in future, it won't be far from King's Denton.'

'You're thinking of your parents?'

'Partly. Dad's retirement has made me think it's time I thought more of them and less of my career. I've been wondering why Aunt Isobel left me her house and I have this feeling, call it sixth sense or something equally weird, that she knew I was looking for a place to put down roots. Does that sound surprising, even ridiculous to you, Cal?'

'I know you and your aunt were very close, and no matter what her reasoning, she left a safe mooring place for you.'

He slipped an arm round her waist, pressed his lips to her forehead.

'You're cold. Let's go,' he said in a whisper.

'Just another few minutes, Cal. It's so wonderfully peaceful here.'

Her mother frequently reminded her that all this would one day be Cal's and there wasn't a young woman who wouldn't jump at the chance to become mistress of Denton Park Hall.

'I'll try your stepping stones barefoot when the water's warmer, July or August next year,' she said openly.

'You could be living in London by then,' he replied unexpectedly.

'London? What would I be doing there?'

'Some sweet-talking art dealer might persuade you.'

'Wrong on both counts. I don't persuade easily, and Giles is not the sweet-talking type. He's a good, sincere man, the kind of caring friend to have around in a crisis. Ask your sister about him and she'll tell you what a tower of strength Giles Shepherd has been to us.'

'So you have no thought about living in London with him?'

'I'm enjoying our conversation enormously, Cal, but I'm also getting progressively colder, so could we head in the direction of the studio and a hot cup of tea?'

Cal smiled.

'Come here, I'll keep you warm until you answer my question,' he said quietly, slipping his arms around her and hugging her close.

'You think I would live with Giles? I'm the marrying kind, Cal. I believe wholeheartedly in good, old-fashioned responsibility and commitment, being married in St Margaret's with all my friends and family. Are you saying you didn't already know that?'

Gently, he took her face in his hands, let his lips slowly work their way across her cheek to fasten on her lips. And though he loosened his hold on her, his gaze held hers.

'I know all there is to know about you. Just needed to hear you say it.'

'Why?' Mel asked, trying to catch her breath and control her thundering heartbeat. 'Cal, you're confusing our relationship. I'm not one of your girlfriends.'

'Then why did you just kiss me like that?'

She felt herself blush.

'Couldn't avoid it. You had a stranglehold on me.'

Cal was still laughing when they reached Briar Rose Cottage and Mel spotted Joshua working at his computer, and waved. She had calmed down considerably by the time they reached Tessa's studio.

'Sorry I'm late, Tessa. My fault, I wanted to walk along the riverbank and see Cal's handiwork.'

'That's all right. Are you staying for a cup of tea, Cal? Just give me a minute to put these brushes away and I'll put on the kettle. Oh, and Giles has been on the phone, wondering why he couldn't get you, Mel, but I said you'd probably be on your way here. Anyway, he can't make it this weekend, but he'll be here next Friday.'

'Sis, I'll skip the tea and girl talk if it's about Mel's army of male admirers,' Cal said, sliding a wicked grin in Melanie's direction.

'Oh, Cal, how could you? You know Mel better than that.'

'I thought I did, but she's being mighty secretive about one of them.'

'What's wrong with him now?' Tessa murmured, watching him leave.

'Don't ask. Probably has too much stuff on his mind at the moment.'

'His expansion plans are exciting, Mel, but he could be biting off more than he can chew with the Newcastle venture. There's something bothering him, but he's not willing to talk about it to anyone, even me. Mother has never seen him so down in the dumps and thinks it must be serious. Did you know he turned down an invitation to the local Chamber of Commerce Ball at the Corn Exchange? Mother is very disappointed, but what's worse is Cal knowing the proceeds are for the hospital's new scanner. And what did he mean about you being secretive? Come to that, why is he sauntering by the river and not in his office or a courtroom at this time of day? I'm telling you, Mel, my brother's recent behaviour is peculiar.'

'I think you're over-reacting, Tessa, but what do I know about men? Anyway, how did your baby check-up go?'

'I'm fine.'

Tessa looked at her watch.

'I must collect James from school, so I'll give you a lift home and I hope your meeting goes well on Friday. I'm sure you're doing the right thing.'

'I know I am. I've been wavering about a lot of things, but my roller-coaster years, not knowing which foreign country I'd be working in next, changing that kind of life, I'm sure about.'

'Good. C'mon, Mel, get your coat and we'll pick up super scallywag.'

That Friday, the early-morning drizzle developed into a steady downpour as lunchtime approached. Quickly glancing at the dark-grey sky, Mel ran to the car, telling herself there was nothing to be nervous about, that bad weather could not possibly be any kind of ill omen. She was having a pub lunch with a man, albeit the big white chief, but although all-powerful, her boss was pleasant enough if shrewd, could be brutally frank, and had an extremely irreverent sense of humour.

An hour later, Mel pushed open the door of The Windmill and a wave of warm air, laughter and general noise from the saloon bar greeted her. Mel slipped her coat off, hung it on a pair of lethal-looking antlers and joined the madly beckoning group at the far end of the bar.

'Hi, Mel. What would you like to drink?'

She smiled. They sounded like a well-rehearsed group chorus.

'This is my pleasure,' another voice

chimed in, one she instantly recognised and turning, Mel found herself in one of her burly driver's bear hugs. 'It's true, then, you're really chucking this game in, Mel?'

'I came today specifically to talk to Tim about my decision. It wasn't an easy one to make, Pete.'

'We've been through too much together in the past for me to think a decision like this would be an easy one for you. As long as you're absolutely sure this is what you want. But whatever you decide, Mel, I hope you're not deserting us altogether.'

'Look out,' someone stage-whispered, 'here comes the organ-grinder.'

'What would you like to eat, Mel? I'm having the cottage pie,' Tim said pulling out a chair at the nearest table for her.

'The ham salad looks good,' she replied, feeling less sure of herself by the minute.

'Well, you're going to quit your job, but not altogether, surely? You're not expecting a baby, are you?' he began.

Feeling her confidence ebb slowly, she shook her head.

'I just think it's time I settled in one place for a while. And my mind is made up,' she added hastily before he could entice her with another of his plum foreign trips, as he liked to label them.

'There are other avenues we could explore,' he began, watching her face, thinking she looked nervous.

'What have you in mind?' she asked quietly.

'I've been mulling over a job in the studios.'

'Is there a vacancy?'

His loud burst of laughter made heads turn in their direction.

'That's what I like about you, Melanie, your reticence,' he teased, raising a forkful of cottage pie to his lips. 'There'll be one shortly.'

She repressed a laugh.

'Sack someone for their reticence, did you?'

'The lady in question is expecting a

baby and intends being a full-time mother, so you would be slotting into that niche, Mel.'

'I'm surprised and grateful for your offer.'

'As long as you don't thank me. You've earned it and it was unanimously agreed that there is no-one more capable or deserving. Take a week or two to think about it and let me know.'

Driving back to King's Denton, Mel felt honoured to have been offered such a sought-after appointment, yet it did have an expensive downside. Commuting to Newcastle each day meant buying a new car. Then there was a complete new wardrobe to find. Any self-respecting charity shop would turn its nose up at her present gear, so it looked as if a serious talk with the bank manager was a must, and very soon she told herself, noticing Calvert Robson's car in her driveway.

'That must've been an interesting lunch, Mel. It's nearly time for dinner.

How did your meeting go?'

'Better than I expected. I didn't want anyone to feel that I was letting them down, but I needn't have worried. In a weird way they all seemed to understand how I felt.'

'Were you offered anything else?'

Mel couldn't hide her smile, knowing instinctively Cal thought she should be offered a worthwhile job after her years with the company.

'I was. Will you help me choose a reliable, small, inexpensive car?'

Cal took her hand in his.

'I might do that if you tell me what's behind your urgent need for a car.'

'It's time I stopped borrowing other people's,' she began, wondering how long he had been waiting here for her.

'Well? Really, Mel, you really are the most aggravating female it has ever been my misfortune to meet. You do know that!'

She looked up at his dear face and thought her cat-and-mouse game unfair under the cold, damp circumstances.

'It'll be warmer inside, Cal.'

And later, when she told him about the television job she'd been offered in the new year, he took a step forward and swung her into his arms.

'This is good news and means no more travelling. That boss of yours hasn't attached strings to his offer?' he asked, looking sceptical.

'No strings, Cal. He knows me too well for that.'

'We'll have to celebrate. This means the end of your dangerous assignments. Your mother'll sleep easier in her bed after hearing this news and I, well, this makes life simpler all round. You'll be home and, yes, you'll need a car.'

'I suppose, with the Christmas holiday looming, I'd better start looking around, but I'll have a chat with the bank manager first.'

'Don't you think a talk with your father would be advisable?'

Mel's smile was rueful. It was sound advice, and her parents had been so good to their only child. Perhaps she could now include them more in her life. She guessed her rating in the good-daughter stakes would be fairly near the bottom of the pile, with no-one to blame but herself. Her career had come first and how relentlessly she had pursued it, sacrificing in the process a marriage, home and the kind of family life her parents would have preferred for her.

'You know my father, Cal. He would hate his little girl borrowing money and would automatically offer me whatever I needed, but I don't want that.'

'His little girl being too independent to accept a helping hand from her loving father, who would rather go out of her way to deprive him of the pleasure of being there for her when she needed him?'

Cal's cutting words pulled her up sharply. She stared at him, hurt and angry. At the shrill sound of the telephone, she hurried into the hall both to answer it and hide the tears glistening in her eyes from a man who plainly had an incredibly low opinion of her. The call was from Tessa.

'Hi, Tessa, how d'you feel today?'

'Very fat, slow and useless.'

'You don't have to be pregnant for fat, slow and useless, Tessa. I have all three on a regular basis,' Mel replied, glad to hear Tessa's ripple of laughter, without an inkling that Cal was standing beside her until his hand turned her face towards him, the pad of his thumb gently wiping a tear from her cheek, his lips whispering in her ear, 'Sorry, angel. Didn't mean to upset you.'

She laid a cautionary hand on his chest and swallowed hard.

'Er, yes, Tessa. Right. I'll call at the studio and tell you all about it later today.'

Slowly, she replaced the receiver.

'Today has been emotionally draining, a catalyst of sorts, so that you must excuse my unusual behaviour, Cal'

She smiled at him.

'So what's your excuse for, among other things, not going to the charity ball at the corn exchange?'

He gazed at her, puzzled.

'What other things?'

'If your latest girlfriend had dumped you, then I could understand these tales I've been told about your grumpiness, but I know you're exceptionally busy at the office, and searching for suitable premises in Newcastle must be a frustrating business.'

'But not half as frustrating as another project I'm working on!' Surprised, Mel touched his arm.

'Is it something you can talk about?'

'Oh, I'll get around to it, but at the moment, you've enough on your mind. There's the decision about working in television studios. That'll be a radical change for you, Mel, and then there's the bigger one about your London boyfriend.'

★ ★ ★

She blamed it on an inborn cantankerousness and, from way back in time,

146

could still hear her mother say, 'If that little Calvert Robson doesn't get what he wants immediately, he'll hold out and vex his mother until she can stand it no longer and the little toad gets his determined way.'

When she heard the front door shut behind him with a resounding thud, Mel muttered, 'So what's new?'

She laughed. If he wasn't getting his own way about something nowadays, she doubted his mother could solve the problem or necessarily have a clue about anything troubling her son. He'd certainly side-tracked her offer of a friendly, sympathetic ear, cleverly swinging the conversation to her new job and then that crazy taunt. What had he against Giles Shepherd, for goodness' sake?

Given Cal's track record, if she didn't know better, she'd think he was jealous of Giles. But if she thought that, she risked making a complete fool of herself with Cal, as she'd done in the past.

'Once bitten,' she murmured, heading for the kitchen.

The following Friday, after buying a black, seductively short dress for the hospital charity do, she called at Juniper Cottage to show her mother what a fine sense of fashion sense lay hidden beneath the boots and camouflage jacket her mother had, on many occasions, warned would seriously reduce any girl's chance of attracting a man.

'It's late. Dad not back from the office yet?'

'He's working late on a criminal case. You'll stay for a meal?' Mel licked her lips.

'It smells good, Mum. Steak and kidney?'

Emily Sinclair laughed.

'I thought today cold enough for what your father calls a proper dinner, and before I forget to tell you, Calvert has changed his mind and bought two tickets for our hospital dance. I did ask his mother whom he was taking, and would you believe when she asked him the same question, well, he wasn't

148

exactly forthcoming.'

'What did he say?' Mel asked quietly.

'His actual words were, it was for him to know and we nosey ex-nursing sisters to find out. Well, Mel, you know I love Calvert Robson as if he was my own, but at times he can be so irritating.'

When Mel's laughter died, she held out a large carrier bag and said, 'Tell me what you think of that.'

Emily raised the dress for inspection and gazing at the fine shoestring shoulder straps echoed, 'What do I think of it? It's perfectly lovely, pet, but you'll catch pneumonia in it. Still, the material's so beautifully soft and feminine, you're going to look like a woman in this, and anyway, antibiotics work amazingly well these days,' she added with a broad smile.

'Who is on antibiotics?' Harvey Sinclair demanded, surprising them and first kissing his wife then his daughter's cheek.

'I was teasing Mel about her new

dress for the hospital dance.'

Mel thought her father looked tired.

'Come and sit down, Daddy. You surely don't have to work such long hours.'

'We're busy just now but, hopefully, it won't be for long. And if it wasn't for Cal starting work at the crack of dawn each day, I really would be over-stretched. He takes so much off my hands, Mel, but can't do everything, not with this Newcastle project to get under way.'

'Has he mentioned whom he's taking to the Corn Exchange next week, dear?' Emily asked in a contrived, disinterested tone, making Mel smile.

'He didn't, dear. We haven't had much time for social conversation of any kind for a few days, but I know he's not seeing anyone.'

Wonders never ceasing occurred to her, but she made no comment.

'What about you, Mel? Made your mind up yet?'

She sighed.

'I'm working on it, but if I make this job change I need to buy a car and a load of new stuff, clothes and things.'

'You'll be permanently in the limelight and, in your case, a whole new wardrobe will be essential, but you can use my little car, Mel, if you're worried about money.'

'Thanks, Mum, but it's time I had a car of my own.'

Over the gold rim of his spectacles, Harvey gazed at his daughter.

'Did you have any special car in mind, dear?'

'Heavens, no. More like four reliable wheels to get me to Newcastle and back each day. Calvert has offered to help me to chose a small, inexpensive model, but even then I'll need a bank loan.'

Her father smiled indulgently at her.

'I would love to help you out, Mel, and my terms would be better.'

'You mean it? But it would have to be a loan.'

Having anticipated her independent reaction, his smile broadened.

'A bona fide business arrangement, Mel. Leave it with me.'

'Thanks, I'll feel better with you handling it,' she told him, kissing his cheek, at the same time wondering how Cal came to know so much about her thoughts and feelings, and if she had sounded annoyingly independent about buying a car, what gave him the right to rebuke her in that high-and-mighty manner, thinking he had some God-given right to remind her of her filial obligations.

'So, assuming you accept this television job, you haven't given any thought to living nearer the studios?' her father enquired quietly.

'You mean Newcastle? Working there will be great, but you know King's Denton is where I've always loved coming back to. Dad, this is home.'

'And I think if you work there and live here, you'll have the best of both worlds, Melanie' her mother said. 'You'll certainly have more chance of meeting more interesting people in Newcastle.'

152

With a nod and a smile for her mother Mel guessed it was time she changed the subject.

'I have a conscience about appropriating your car, Mum, and if it's possible to start looking for one of my own next week, I'll feel less guilty.'

'It's so good to see you back home with us, having you borrow my little car's not something to concern yourself about. Keep it as long as you need it,' her mother replied, her thoughts still on the golden opportunities sure to be waiting for an attractive television presenter in a big, vibrant city like Newcastle just teeming with interesting, unmarried men.

It was growing dark when Melanie left Juniper Cottage, mulling over Tim Bradshaw's job offer. She visualised herself working in Newcastle where she'd still be reporting on the news, beginning to reckon the advantages could outweigh all other criteria by a mile.

By the time she arrived at her garden

gate, Mel's mind was made up. She would accept the evening slot, report on the news as she had before, only this time from the safety of a chair in a television studio. It was, she finally decided, too good an opportunity to turn down.

First thing the following morning, she phoned Tim Bradshaw's office, thanked him and accepted the job. Her second call was to her father to tell him she was going to need the new car sooner that she'd thought.

Replacing the receiver, she refused to think of her old job, the carefree lifestyle she had enjoyed these last few years, at times dangerous and frightening, but now, looking to the future, she could congratulate herself on having made a positive, right decision.

Mel was still standing by the phone daydreaming when Tessa rang.

'Giles has just phoned me about a picture he's picking up on Friday and asked if you'd made up your mind about that studio job yet, and I told him you were still dithering.'

'No more. I've just informed the boss I'll be available in the new year.'

'How exciting, Mel. A new beginning for you, but I don't think Giles Shepherd will be impressed. I suspect the new beginning he was hoping for had nothing to do with television studios.'

Mel laughed.

'Rubbish, Tessa, and I don't need another matchmaker, thank you, not with mother eyeing every man still able to walk unaided as prospective husband material,' she teased.

'Actually, the reason I phoned had nothing to do with work. Mother asked me to drop some stuff off at Grandma's place in Newcastle next week and if you came along, we could make a day of it, do some shopping, have lunch somewhere nice. What d'you think?'

'Count me in, Tessa. I need to start getting a few new clothes together and I'm keeping Mum's car till I get my own, so we have transport.'

'Mother wants me to deliver a folding bed and mattress, so it'll have to be the people carrier. It's roomier, more comfortable for me to drive.'

'You're eight months pregnant, Tessa. Shouldn't you be pottering about Briar Rose Cottage, resting each afternoon with everyone dancing attendance on you? I know Mother thinks you're behaving very sensibly, but then, she has this pretty picture of you sitting in your studio doing nothing more energetic than painting pretty pictures.'

'Your mother's a sweet lady and what's more, she's right. I have done a lot of painting recently, but miss an opportunity to go to Newcastle simply because I'm pregnant? You know me better than that, Mel.'

Long after their phone conversation, from her sitting-room window, Mel looked across the windswept village green, thinking of how well she knew her friend. She smiled. Tessa could be as incredibly strong-minded as her brother. Her smile widened as Cal's car pulled into the drive and she went to the front door, suspecting her father had been talking.

'Hi, Cal. I've just been talking to Tessa, telling her about my big decision.'

'Your father told me, but that's not why I called. Look, Mel,' he began hesitantly, 'I would like to take you to the hospital charity ball.'

Melanie stared.

'But we always go together.'

'No, we always go in a group, your family and mine, but I'm asking if, this year, I can take you specifically,' he said, gazing intently at her.

Baffled by his request, Mel returned his gaze, feeling reluctant to voice her immediate reaction, yet wanting to ask, 'Why me?'

'I've surprised you, but it's time we changed a few people's misconceptions about us, Mel,' he said quietly, reaching for her hand.

'I thought you'd be too busy to go this year with the Newcastle expansion venture. How's it going?'

'Great,' he replied enthusiastically. 'I've found the premises I've been searching for and after some minor alterations and a bit of redecoration, the old firm should be in business in Newcastle before Easter.'

'You must be delighted.'

'Yeah. When it's all finished, it'll be good to have time for the more everyday things, like breathing normally again,' he said with a wry smile. 'I'm still waiting for your answer, Mel. Will you go to the dance with me?'

'I'd love to,' she replied softly, thinking of the stir it was sure to create.

'Good. So it's a date? And when d'you start this new job?'

'Not until early in the new year. I've decided to buy a car right away, and thanks for offering to help me choose one.'

'Give me time to look at my office diary and we'll go car shopping one day next week.'

★   ★   ★

When they pulled up outside the house, Mel locked her door and couldn't believe the amount of stuff packed in the old car.

'You look as if you're moving house, Tessa.'

'You know Mother. There's everything in those boxes from bottled plums to cream for Grandma's arthritis. Hop in, Mel, and watch your head. That folding bed juts out a bit.'

'Right. We have all day, Tessa, so we'll take everything nice and easy.'

'And there's no need to rush back. Josh is picking little James up from school and they're going to the Hall for tea, so we'll drop this load off at Grandma's place first, then head for the shops.'

Mel wasn't altogether happy about Tessa driving the car, but there was little she could do with her friend saying how much she loved driving. Only when Tessa stopped outside her grandma's house and Mel was actively engaged in the physical work of emptying the car did she stop worrying, and switched to wishing she knew more about pregnancy and childbirth.

By mutual agreement, their shopping spree was interspersed with breaks for coffee, a leisurely lunch and an early tea, when Mel thought it a good idea to get back home before dark. Yet, glancing at Tessa's happy, excited face, Mel smiled and wondered why she had felt so uptight about her.

Nonetheless, it was with sighs of relief that they threw their collection of bags and packages into the car and after fastening seat belts, the girls glanced at each other and simultaneously, burst out laughing.

'We're on our way,' Tessa said, still chuckling as she started the car. 'So you can relax. Your worst fears are not about to be realised, Melanie Sinclair. I'm neither going to give birth on a department store elevator nor a ladies' fashion floor.'

'Sorry, Tessa, I know I've been a bit of a pain today, but what do I know about anything?' Mel replied, feeling unusually pleased to be leaving the traffic-filled streets of Newcastle behind her today.

A pale, wintry sun was setting as they neared the Hall, the road bordering the King's Denton estate little more than a narrow country lane that both girls knew so well, with its high, hawthorn hedge on one side and the ditch on the other. Mel spotted the tractor the instant its front wheels appeared out on the road.

'A tractor, Tessa, from the field. On your right!' she yelled at the top of her voice.

Mel's strident warning immediately jolted Tessa to the expectancy of danger and, gripping the steering wheel, she swerved the car to avoid a collision with the oncoming tractor, but the big vehicle overshot the road, its nearside front wheel ending in the ditch, the bonnet of the car hitting an old tree stump, where it stopped, its smashed radiator hissing steam.

Steadying herself after the impact, Mel heard someone open the driver's door and say, 'Dear God, it's young Tessa and she's unconscious.'

Feeling dazed, Mel fumbled for her seat belt, undid it, picked her bag off her lap and, opening her door, slowly lowered herself into the ditch and crawled along the bank on her hands and knees until she was clear of the car. Gasping for breath, she hauled herself back up the bank and on to the road where she pulled her mobile out of her bag and hit the 999 button.

'This is an emergency. I need an ambulance,' she said.

'It's Melanie, isn't it? Are you all right, lass?'

She saw the tractor driver was one of the estate workers.

'I'm all right, but it's Tessa and her baby I'm worried about. An ambulance is on its way and should be here soon.'

'I'll go to the Hall and tell them what's happened.'

'Thanks, but Calvert should be told

first. I'll phone him,' she said, looking at Tessa, smoothing hair off her face and holding her hand, wanting her to be out of the car and lying flat somewhere, anywhere more natural than in the car. 'You're going to be all right, Tessa. They'll probably want to keep you in hospital for a day or two, do some tests and that sort of thing, but you're as tough as old boots and, after all, we've been in worse scrapes than this,' Mel told her with tears streaming down her face.

By the last rays of the setting sun, Mel phoned Calvert's office and when she heard his voice, she said, 'Cal,' and broke down, couldn't utter another word for the sobs that shook her body.

'Tell me what's wrong, Mel,' he said quietly.

'It's Tessa . . . accident in the estate lane.'

'Have you called an ambulance?'

'Yes, and I'll go to hospital with her. I won't leave her.'

'I know you won't leave her and I'll

be with you at the hospital. Hold on, Mel. You'll see, she'll be fine,' he said, not knowing exactly what had happened, yet instinctively knowing it was serious.

No sooner had the ambulance stopped in the lane than the paramedics had Tessa out of the car, on a stretcher and into the ambulance, so carefully and with such speed, Mel couldn't believe their efficiency.

'She looks better, her face not quite so pale,' she murmured, wanting to believe her dear friend wasn't badly hurt.

At that moment, Tessa's eyes opened.

'I bumped my head.'

Mel turned to the paramedic.

'She's going to be all right, isn't she?'

'We're taking good care of her. It's you who should be taking things easy. We don't want you flaking out on us as well.'

Tessa gave the paramedic a withering look.

'My friend doesn't flake out in

emergencies. She's not the type, and it was her quiet thinking and speedy action that brought you here so rapidly.'

Amused, Mel was relieved to hear there couldn't be much wrong with her, not when she was politely putting the paramedic in his place. And if a bit shaken, Tessa was telling herself she felt all right when a searing pain shot through her and she grabbed the ambulance man's arm.

'It must be the baby. That was a contraction,' she gasped.

'Great,' the man replied casually. 'Then it's just as well we're almost at the hospital. You'll be in the maternity unit in a few more minutes.'

'Phone Josh, Mel, but don't tell him about the accident yet, just that the baby has started.'

Half an hour later, Mel was in the waiting-room feeling totally inadequate, wishing she'd been allowed to stay with Tessa until Josh arrived. She gazed at her best black suit, now wet and smelling of stagnant ditchwater, the mud on her legs mingling with drops of blood from her grazed knees, yet Tessa and her baby were her only concern.

Cal burst into the waiting-room, stopped, glanced at Mel's dirt and tear-streaked face and said, 'Mel, you're hurt!'

'I have phoned Josh to tell him the baby's coming.'

'I brought him here and he's with Tessa now, but look,' he said, pulling the nearest chair towards her, 'we'll wait a while, then I'll take you home. Did you know you have a dirty face, sweetheart?'

'What about the tractor driver, Cal? He looked badly shocked.'

'Jake's all right. My father's with him, so don't distress yourself, Mel,' he said, guessing she'd had just about all she could take today and should be at home, not hanging about here looking totally shattered.

He took her hand in his and it was on the tip of his tongue to suggest they went home now and came back later, when the door opened and Josh appeared with a huge grin on his face. Mel was on her feet in a flash.

'Is Tessa all right?'

'She's fine, Mel. We have a little girl and she's beautiful,' Josh said, his face beaming, but his emotion evident in his unusually shaky voice.

'Really? Oh, Cal, isn't that wonderful news? I'm so happy,' Mel said unsteadily, paying no heed to the tears streaming down her cheeks or that she was on her toes, her arms around Cal's neck and she was kissing him.

Cal joined in with his congratulations.

'It's terrific news. Give Tessa our love, Josh. Tell her we'll be back after she has had a rest. Come on, Mel, I know this calls for a celebration, but that can come later. After your hair-raising adventure today, you need a large drink, something to calm your nerves.'

'What I need is a long soak in a hot bath,' she replied, thinking that over the past few hours she had visualised every possible injury Tessa and her baby might have sustained.

Yet the bump they'd had seemed to have done little more than precipitate the earlier arrival of the baby. And as much as she would love to see them, they would have to wait.

Cal soon stopped the car outside her door and Mel said self-consciously, 'Sorry about that kiss at the hospital. I hope you weren't too embarrassed. I got a bit carried away.'

'I've been thinking, Mel. We should both have that drink and while I'm in the house, I could help you with things such as running your bath, tucking you into bed and suchlike.'

Mel laughed.

'Thanks for the lift home and, tempting though your offer is, you've probably guessed I'm not in a very sociable mood so I'll just call it a day. Good-night Cal.'

Gently, he ran the back of his hand across a bruise on her cheek.

'You've had a nasty shock and need a good, long sleep. I'll call and see you sometime tomorrow,' he said tenderly.

7

Melanie woke with a start, turned her head in the direction of the bedside clock and dived out of bed. She should've been to see Tessa two hours ago, she thought, running to the bathroom, turning on the shower and inspecting her sore, scratched knees.

She wondered how she acquired the bruise on her right hip and, for some obscure reason, remembered last night and Cal's offer of help. Mel chuckled softly. Still, as annoying as Cal could be at times, she couldn't fault him in an emergency. He was reliable, always had been, except perhaps on the odd occasion when his mind was on other things, such as a new girlfriend.

After a quick slice of toast and a cup of tea, Mel slipped into her coat, slung her bag over her shoulder, opened her door and stopped.

'Good morning. This is a surprise. How are you, Giles?' she exclaimed.

'Good morning, Mel. I should've called you, but didn't get back to Newcastle until late last night. What've you been up to lately?'

'Tessa had her baby yesterday, a little girl, and I was just on my way to the maternity unit to see them. Why don't we go to the hospital together? Tessa would expect me to ask you,' she added hastily.

'Then, yes, if you're sure. I'd love to see Tessa and her new baby and I promise not to talk business. And it's good to see you again, Mel.'

'Hold on a minute, Giles. I must take my camera.'

Luckily, there were no visitors at Tessa's bedside, the only things surrounding her friend being large bouquets of flowers, overflowing vases of yellow and red roses, a pot of pink African violets and a posy of winter jasmine, their collective scents like an exotic perfume.

'No wonder all the florists in King's

Denton have sold out,' Mel teased, bending to kiss Tessa's cheek. 'Who's a clever girl then?'

'Oh, Mel, don't you think my daughter's absolutely perfect?'

A lovely, healthy baby she indeed was, yet gazing into the cot at the pink-faced, sleeping infant, Mel's thoughts were on the car accident, the shock and fear she'd felt for both her friend and her baby.

'She's perfectly lovely.'

'This is a pleasant surprise, Giles. Has Mel told you about the bump we had in the car yesterday?'

Mel sat listening to Tessa relay in graphic detail what was beginning to sound more like a jolly escapade they'd had rather than an incident, the potential consequences of which still sent shivers down her spine. Looking towards the door, Mel saw Cal, and her thoughts instantly switched to how good he looked today, how kind and considerate he had been yesterday and how the frisson she felt at that moment had nothing whatsoever to do with yesterday's nasty experience, but another, entirely different personal and infinitely more pleasurable feeling.

She felt his hand on her shoulder, looked up and said, 'Hi, Cal.'

Cal kissed Tessa's cheek.

'And how's my little sister doing?'

'I'm fine and so is the baby, Cal. She looks like you.'

'Poor wee thing,' Mel's sympathetic whisper made Giles laugh.

'What d'you think of my baby niece then, Giles? But more importantly, have you and Josh decided on a name for her yet, Tessa?'

'Yes, Cal, just an hour or so ago, Josh and I finally decided to call her Melanie Cecilia Maitland. Cecilia after Miss Calvert Denton, but Melanie after you, Mel.'

Mel stared at her, dumbfounded.

'You're not serious!'

'We're calling her after you because of your prompt action yesterday which saved me and my baby, and they were the gynaecologist's words, not mine.'

'Well, I'm flattered and honoured, but what I did yesterday, Tessa, anybody would've done given the same hairy set of circumstances.'

'And when you do her portrait, Tessa, I'll show it in the London gallery,' Giles chipped in proudly.

'I have two pictures for you in the studio and if you want to see them straight away, Mel knows where they are.'

'The two leopard cubs' water colours in the parlour of The Lodge?' Mel asked.

'They're the ones, Mel, but I'm not sure if animal drawings are still popular these days.' Tessa shrugged. 'What do you think, Giles?'

'I'll take a look at them later. And what's this I've been hearing about your new business premises in Newcastle, Cal? I'm told they're palatial. When are you moving in?'

'There's quite a bit of work still to be done and it's frustrating having to wait, but if too slow for me, progress is being made and the builders have an end of the year deadline to complete, or else.'

Mel thought Giles made it sound as if Cal was taking over the Newcastle branch of the law firm himself, and while she longed to ask who would run the new offices, she decided there was little point in doing so when she'd known all along that he wanted to carry on working in King's Denton, had faithfully promised her father that he would never quit the old firm in their home town.

After Mel had used her last film on Tessa and the baby, she packed her camera away, kissed Tessa's cheek and promised to call and see her the next day.

'I'll get those pictures from The Lodge for you, Giles, if Tessa tells me where to find the key.'

'In my bag, and, Mel, if you can spare some time for little James. The first question he asked me this morning was how long I was going to stay away from home.'

Tessa gave her friend a knowing look, and Mel immediately got the message. She remembered well the day Tessa had packed for their trip to America and Josh's little boy wouldn't leave her side, asking if she was leaving him for always. Tessa had wept after promising the unhappy child that she would never leave him, that she loved him. And how could she adequately explain to such a small child that his mother had also loved him, but she had been a very sick lady?

Josh had talked to his little boy, tried to explain why his real mother was no longer with them, unfortunately without much success. Mel understood the situation.

'Don't worry, Tessa, I'll keep an eye on him,' she promised.

As James grew older, he would appreciate his good fortune, Mel mused, would realise that Tessa was a loving, caring mother. He'd appreciate and love her in return, and with the addition of a bonny baby daughter, the Maitlands were indeed a whole family.

'Must get back to the grindstone,' Cal announced, pushing back his chair. 'I think little Mel's a beaut, Tessa, and the big one's not so bad either,' he quipped with a sly wink for Mel.

'The audacity of that brother of yours,' Mel responded, smiling as she watched him stride away. 'Mother said she'd come in to see you later, so we'd better let you get some rest. Come on, Giles, we'll get those pictures for you, and no, Tessa, I won't forget about James.'

'Thanks for coming, Giles, and it's good to know your foot is healing.'

'Discarding the crutches and walking more or less normally is a huge bonus, Tessa.'

As they left the hospital, the rain was pelting down and they hurried to the car with Giles moving at a surprising pace with the aid of a smart, ebony walking stick.

'Tessa's delighted with her baby,' Giles said, starting the engine.

'But a mite peeved about missing the hospital dance at the Corn Exchange this year.'

'I won't be dancing for a few weeks, Mel, but I'd like to take you,' he said, swinging the car on to the Denton Park Estate and pulling up outside The Lodge.

'I'm sorry, Giles. I've already accepted an invitation.'

'Calvert got there first, huh? I might've known. You two always seem to be at daggers drawn, yet I get a distinct impression that you're closer than either of you cares to admit.'

'You're very intuitive. Cal and I go back a long way. We were almost brought up together and always close, with hindsight, too close and too young. He wasn't ready for a serious relationship and I was wrapped up in my journalistic career, so we went separate ways.'

'Yet an interested onlooker can see

that you're more than friends, and no longer too young, so what are you waiting for, Mel?'

'The answer is me. I have some very quaint ideas on this subject, need to be sure that a man is ready to settle down with a woman and accept the requisite commitment. The other big drawback is, I believe in marriage, having children and all that old-fashioned kind of thing.'

Mel's smile was rueful.

'Time to take a look at those leopard cubs,' Giles murmured thoughtfully, figuring that Mel was in love and Cal didn't know what a lucky guy he was.

While Giles stood at the parlour window studying the two water colours, Mel was pleased she had told him something of her relationship with Cal. She knew Giles liked her, suspected he was biding his time, perhaps hoping for encouragement from her before pushing their friendship further. But despite having grown fond of him, that was something she couldn't do.

'Well, what d'you think of the leopards?'

'Your friend is amazing, Mel. These cubs are so real they almost jump out at you. Tessa's talent really is incredible and rare, when there's not another member of her family with any artistic talent whatsoever, or even remotely interested in the subject.'

'That's not surprising. Her father was a policeman, her mother, like mine, a nurse, and along with Cal, all probably too busy earning a living to stop and wonder if they could even draw a straight line.'

Giles laughed quietly at her practical reasoning, yet had to agree that it took more than raw talent to acquire Tessa's finishing touches.

'Tell Tessa I'm taking her cubs, Mel, and if you promise not to spend the whole evening with Cal, I'll come to that dance next week anyway.'

On the evening of the dance, Mel zipped up her black silky dress, feeling excited at the thought of Cal calling for her. She hadn't told anyone, not even her parents. She couldn't bear the thought of her mother's exaggerated interpretation of her daughter having an evening out with an old friend.

Her mother would be surprised to see them together at this particular dance again, and although too polite to allude to it this evening, her curiosity would nevertheless be aroused, her unspoken questions hanging in the air as redolent as my French perfume, Mel mused.

She heard his familiar tap at the door and ran to open it.

'You look beautiful this evening, Mel.'

'Thanks, Cal. I thought the dress a bit flashy for the Corn Exchange but decided to wear it anyway. When I showed it to Mother, she reckoned I'd be catching a man or pneumonia in it, a moot point.'

When they stopped laughing, Cal said, 'Your mother would, but then she doesn't know you've already caught your man.'

Guessing he was referring to Giles Shepherd, and refusing to be drawn into an argument on any subject this evening, she stayed silent.

After parking the car in the market square, they were approaching the ancient, brilliantly-lit and tastefully-revamped Corn Exchange, when they met Giles and and old acquaintance of them all, Cressy Slater.

'It's wonderful news about Tessa's baby, Mel, but such a shame she won't be here tonight.'

'She's a bit peeved about missing this one, Cressy, but looking forward to the St Valentine's Ball.'

When the two men joined mutual friends in the foyer, Mel and Cressy went to the lady's cloakroom together. Mel was depositing her coat with the attendant when Cressy spoke up.

'I was surprised to hear Calvert is leaving King's Denton to set up his own business in Newcastle. Of course, he's a young man and no doubt ambitious, so I can understand him closing the small King's Denton business down and choosing to work in the city, especially now that you're father's on the verge of retiring.'

'It's true Cal is opening new offices in Newcastle, Cressy, but he has no intention of leaving King's Denton to work there.'

'Oh, but he is. Tessa told me just a couple of weeks ago all about her brother's plan which I thought made sound business sense.'

'Tessa told you?' Mel asked, unwilling to believe her, yet hadn't that same uncertainty crossed her mind more than once lately.

Then again, Cal had never once uttered a word about hiring staff for that building. Totally mystified, she took a deep breath, told herself to stay calm, and trying to control her simmering anger, she left Cressy.

'The band sounds good, Mel. D'you want to dance or say hello to our parents first,' Cal asked.

Looking at him, despite what she had

just heard, she still felt the same reflexive quickening of her pulse.

'I'd like to say hello to your mother, Cal. I haven't had a chance to congratulate her on becoming a grand-mother and she looks a very glamorous one tonight.'

'Yeah, but not half as lovely as you,' he responded, slipping his arm around her waist as they approached their parent's table.

'You made it, Cal,' Harvey said with a smile for his business partner.

'I don't know how. The traffic out of Newcastle was bumper to bumper for what seemed countless miles.'

Taking a deep breath to steady herself, Mel cleared her throat and said, 'Well, you won't have that trouble much longer, not once your new offices open and you're working in Newcastle. I suppose it will be more convenient for you to live there.'

'What?'

Cal stared at her, saw she was angry and took her hand.

'They're playing a foxtrot, so let's dance, Mel,' he commanded, tugging her towards the dance floor.

'Of all the scheming, unreliable men I have ever met, Calvert Robson, but forget about my feelings. How could you do this to my father?'

'I don't understand, Mel. You'll have to unravel this for me.'

'Cressy Slater told me that it's your intention to close the King's Denton offices of Sinclair & Robson down once my father has retired. If you are moving to Newcastle permanently, I think that's a despicable betrayal of my father's trust and while I don't want to believe you're a man of such little integrity, how can I do otherwise when it was Tessa who told Cressy? But if it's true, Cal, that really will be the end of our friendship,' she told him shakily, her eyes awash with tears.

'There are some seriously crossed wires here,' he said in a low, tense voice. 'And more than anyone, I'm to blame. I should've told you long before now, but you seemed to have enough worries at the time, were anxious about giving up your old job, then wondering about taking the one at the Newcastle studios. Look, we can't talk here. Come back to the table and we'll find somewhere quiet.'

They were alone at the table when Mel said, 'You are working there?'

'Yes, I am, I'll have to, but only for three weeks. After that time, the two solicitors I've chosen will be free to start work in the new offices. Your father knows this and I've found a good man to assist him until I come back. You didn't trust me, Mel,' he accused her, his dark eyes, usually so benign, as cold as flint.

'And you're not selling the King's Denton office then?'

'How could I when it's not mine to sell? Your father still owns that.'

'I don't know what to say except that I felt so miserably hurt and unhappy that everyone knew you were moving away from King's Denton except me.'

'I'm sorry, Mel. The date for moving into the Newcastle offices has been shifting from week to week, but that's no excuse. I should've told you what was happening myself.'

'And I should've known you wouldn't do anything so deceitful, Cal, so I'm as much to blame.'

They were alone at the table talking quietly together when Sally and Ben Robson, then Emily and Harvey Sinclair came back to their seats at the table.

'The trouble is, Mel, you have never completely trusted me,' Cal reminded her, seemingly oblivious to either his parents or hers.

'Well, you can blame that on your never-ending string of girlfriends. Those affairs of yours didn't exactly engender my trust in you,' she retorted, apparently also unaware of their amused parents.

'They were not affairs. I didn't love them, not as I love you, nor did I want any single one of them to become the mother of my children. It's you I love, Mel, always have and always will.'

'And I love you, Cal. With me, it was never anyone but you.'

He gripped her hand, got to his feet and tugged her into his arms.

'Does this mean you'll marry me?'

'Yes, Cal,' she murmured happily.

'We've wasted enough time, so let's make it soon, angel.'

'And not before time,' Harvey chipped in, smiling at his daughter's flushed, happy face.

'I'll say a hearty amen to that, Harv,' Ben added, sounding delighted.

Sally and Emily glanced at each other, both jubilant, their smiles as wide as the Tyne Bridge.

THE END

We do hope that you have enjoyed reading this large print book.

Did you know that all of our titles are available for purchase?

We publish a wide range of high quality large print books including:
Romances, Mysteries, Classics
General Fiction
Non Fiction and Westerns

Special interest titles available in large print are:
The Little Oxford Dictionary
Music Book, Song Book
Hymn Book, Service Book

Also available from us courtesy of Oxford University Press:
Young Readers' Dictionary
(large print edition)
Young Readers' Thesaurus
(large print edition)

For further information or a free brochure, please contact us at:
Ulverscroft Large Print Books Ltd.,
The Green, Bradgate Road, Anstey,
Leicester, LE7 7FU, England.
Tel: (00 44) **0116 236 4325**
Fax: (00 44) **0116 234 0205**

When merchandise is stolen from the shop where Isabel Hindley works, she and the other shop assistants are under suspicion. So when Lady Yettington is observed going out of the shop without paying for goods, Isabel accuses her ladyship of theft, making her nephew, Charles Yettington, furious. But things are more complicated when Lady Yettington is put under surveillance, and more merchandise goes missing. Isabel and Charles plan to find out who is responsible.

THE KINDLY LIGHT

Valerie Holmes

Annie Darton's life was happiness itself, living with her father, the lighthouse keeper of Gannet Rock, until an accident changed their lives forever. Forced to move, Annie's path crosses with the attractive stranger, Zachariah Rudd. Shrouded in mystery, undoubtedly hiding something, he becomes steadily more involved in Annie's life, especially when the new lighthouse keeper is murdered. Annie finds herself drawn into the mysteries around her. Only by resolving the past can she look to the future, whatever the cost!

LOVE AND WAR

Joyce Johnson

Alison Dowland is about to marry her childhood sweetheart, Joe, when his regiment is recalled to battle, and American soldiers descend on the tiny Cornish harbour of Porthallack to prepare for the D-day landings. Excitement is high as the villagers prepare to welcome their allies, but to her dismay, Alison falls in love with American Chuck Bartlett. Amidst an agonising personal decision, she is also caught up in espionage, endangering herself and her sister.

OPPOSITES ATTRACT

Chrissie Loveday

Jeb Marlow was not happy to trust his life to the young pilot who was to fly him through a New Zealand mountain range in poor weather. What was more, the pilot was a girl. Though they were attracted, Jacquetta soon realised they lived in different worlds; he had a champagne lifestyle, dashing around the world, and she helped run an isolated fruit farm in New Zealand. Could they ever have any sort of relationship or would their differences always come between them?

WEB OF EVASION

Glenis Wilson

When Lara Denton's unmarried mother dies in a horrific horse-riding accident, she is brought up by her only relative, Grandma Emma. However, when Lara becomes a jockey, Emma disinherits her. At twenty-five, disenchanted by the male dominated world of horse racing, Lara decides to return to Bingham and make peace with Emma. Sadly, she had died. Too late, Lara realises nothing is more important than family. But who was her father? Can she unravel the mystery surrounding her birth?

THE SAFE HEART

June Gadsby

Delphine's dream holiday in the South of France turns into a nightmare when she witnesses a murder. Placed in a 'safe house', she is faced with the dilemma of not knowing whom to trust. Handsome Commissaire Paul Dulac, in charge of her safety, would appear to be on the side of the villains. Her new boyfriend, Mark, is not exactly what he seems either. And what is the important evidence they seem to think she possesses?